The man was naked!

Kaley couldn't take her eyes off him as she stood up.

"Hey, missy, are you hurt or has the cat got your tongue?"

The way he was standing there without a shred of embarrassment or modesty confused her. "Would you mind putting on some clothes?"

"Haven't finished my bath yet." But he swept the hat off his head and held it fast at a strategic location.

"You were deliberately exposing yourself." Her voice shook as she took in his chest, covered with a dark mat of curly hair beaded with water droplets. His untanned abdomen and legs had the look of marble, as if every tendon and ropy muscle had been delineated by a sculptor.

He grinned. "Where I've been we don't bathe with our clothes on." Slater caught the tremor in her stance. "Don't take my size into account, missy. I'm not what you're thinking. I've never had call or desire to stay where I'm unwanted, if you know what I mean." He cocked an eyebrow at her.

Her heart began to pump hard. "What utter arrogance. I wasn't thinking—"

His grin lifted, mocking her. "You were, missy, you were."

Dear Reader,

I used to think Christmas was just for children, but now I know Christmas is special for all of us.

Some Christmases ago, H.A. and I found our children scattered about the world and experienced, for the first time, an empty-nest Christmas. I thought, "Gee, what a treat. I don't have to put up a tree, hide presents, cook a mountain of food or wash a thousand dishes." I mailed off gifts, and that was it.

Along about the middle of December I found myself deciding to "just put up a few lights around the front door." They looked a bit lonely, so I added lawn decorations. We had a winter storm and it blew great bunches of mistletoe out of the old oak tree in the front yard. I couldn't let it go to waste. I made a wreath. A friend sent a gift of pecans. I baked pies and cookies.

Meanwhile, the corner where the Christmas tree usually stood looked forlorn and empty. We bought a tree and dug out the dusty boxes of decorations from the back of the closet. Among them were all those lumpy clay Santas, crumbling Play-Do candy canes and construction-paper stockings our children had made and so proudly brought home from school.

H.A. and I curled up on the sofa, sipped hot chocolate and talked of those past Christmases, each recalling some little event that the other had forgotten. We laughed. I cried. It was wonderful. It was Christmas.

There is something magical about Christmas. I know fate and life's events sometimes have a way of submerging that magic, but now I know I can't do without my "Christmas fix."

One of my gifts to myself this year is *A Country Christmas.* It's a gift I want to share with you. And if you think that the event in Slater's life is more miracle than true life, it's not, really. What happens to Slater happened to our own son.

Hugs and Happy Holidays!

Jackie

A Country Christmas

JACKIE WEGER

SILHOUETTE

Sensation

All the characters in this book have no existence outside the imagination of the Author, and have no relation whatsoever to anyone bearing the same name or names. They are not even distantly inspired by any individual known or unknown to the Author, and all the incidents are pure invention.

First published in Great Britain in 1994
by Silhouette Books, Eton House, 18-24 Paradise Road,
Richmond, Surrey TW9 1SR

ISBN 0 373 59276 0

95-9411

Made and printed in Great Britain

Chapter One

Slater Rutledge sat up to his neck in a natural pool fed by a trickling spring. Soapsuds whirled and eddied then went charging downstream. He watched a brown lizard creep along a low-hanging limb and dart its tongue out for a sip of water.

In the distance a twig snapped, gravel rolled, and the forest was suddenly ghostly silent.

Slater tilted his hat back and bit down on his cigar as if the set of his jaw and the angle of his hat contributed to his keen hearing.

His eyes scanned the rock face from which the stream spewed. Above it was a slate run, slick with lichen, and that was the approach of his visitor.

Had to be either a fool or friend, he decided, for the footsteps crunched the slate, announcing the hiker's presence.

A yelp of dismay broke the silence. Gravel and dust came tumbling over the rock face, showering him with shards. Great clumps of soil hit the water and sent up a shower that put out his cigar.

Bloody hell! He moved aside, fully expecting the hiker to come shooting over the lip of the rock face and join him in the shallow pool.

As the debris floated away or settled to the bottom of the pool, he looked up to find a pair of boots hanging over the precipice. A low groan escaped their owner. "Any bones broken?" he called out.

The boots disappeared, replaced by a face looking down over the edge of the rock face. Slater's antennas went on high alert.

It was a nice face consisting of large gray eyes, a pert nose, a lush mouth and a wild mane of dark hair that had escaped its tether. A blue ribbon clung to a few strands and trailed down over her shoulder. He felt a shiver of anticipation.

"Heard you coming from a mile off, missy. Figured if you were that light of step and still making noise, you were friendly. Of course, your entrance is a bit peculiar."

She still didn't speak, and her eyes weren't tracking. Slater sighed inwardly. He'd have to climb the rock face and check her out. She'd probably banged her head in the fall. Shedding water, he rose to his feet.

The hat was all he wore.

Kaley blinked.

The man was deeply tanned from the waist up, his biceps threaded with muscle and accented with colorful tattoos. His chest, covered with a dark mat of curly hair beaded with water droplets, looked a yard wide and was bisected by a long thin scar. His untanned abdomen and legs had the look of marble, as if every tendon and ropy muscle had been delineated by a skilled sculptor.

He was *huge.* He was Poseidon, god of the sea, son of Cronus and Rhea. A mythic being staring her right in the face.

No, she thought, her senses returning full force. He was some weirdo with the idea of playing Tarzan, and practically in her backyard, too.

Slater took the cigar out of his mouth. "Hey, missy, are you hurt, or has the cat got your tongue?"

Kaley realized that the way he was standing there naked without a shred of embarrassment or modesty was confusing her. "Would you mind putting on some clothes?"

"Haven't finished my bath yet." But he swept the hat off his head and held it fast against a strategic location.

"You were deliberately exposing yourself." She could see now that his hair was long, but tied back with a leather thong.

He grinned. "Where I've been we don't bathe with our clothes on. Besides, my momma taught me to always stand when a lady entered the room. What did your momma teach you?"

Kaley's eyes flashed "*How* to be a lady. Ladylike was her pet phrase." She stood up and brushed herself off, discovering both of her elbows had been scraped raw in her slide down the incline.

"Truly, missy?" He put the cigar back in his mouth, chewing it to one side as his glance ranged over her, taking her measure, liking what he saw. "You don't look the type who aspires to be a lady. Nope, you sure don't strike me as a woman of stiff hats, straight seams and a narrow heart.''

''However I strike you, mister, it's obvious you'd have no use for a lady.'' She noticed his hands and shivered. They were large and powerful and brutal-looking.

Slater caught the tremor, studying her gravely for a moment before he spoke, though his gaze included a measure of sexual candor. ''Don't take my size into account, missy. I'm not what you're thinking. I've certainly never had call or desire to stay where I'm unwelcome, if you know what I mean.'' He cocked an eyebrow in her direction.

Her heart began to pump hard. ''What utter arrogance. I wasn't thinking—''

His grin lifted, mocking her. ''You were. I read your eyes, missy. They're talking to me. You were signing to me in soul language. Same as tracking a wild mare. Got to read her sign, know her soul, know what's in her mind to figure what she's gonna do next, where she's going to ground, or what tricks she's up to.''

The peculiar way he spoke caught at her, but she couldn't quite place his accent. ''I can assure you I'm not up to any tricks. I saw your smoke and came up to check it out. *We've* had a dry summer.''

''Do tell. You must be busy as hell, running about these mountains checking every little puff of smoke against the possibility of a forest fire.''

The fire, he saw, burned behind her eyes, which were aflame with inner turmoil. His ego, which was ample but tolerated a stroke now and again, unfolded with satisfaction.

"I don't race to every puff of smoke." She was becoming visibly annoyed. "It's just that yours was so close to our place." It was a fact that she didn't have the wherewithal to run the man off the mountain. And she wasn't sure she wanted to. "I suppose if you're just camping up here, it's okay. But don't overstay your welcome. The sheriff checks this area regularly."

"Does he?"

"Yes, for marijuana growers, transients, people like that."

"I see." Standing, she had drawn about her a barrier of self, but left on display a curious tilt of her head, full breasts and a slender waist that flared into rounded hips. The décolletage of her cotton shirt drew his attention. She had yet to notice that two buttons had been torn away in her tumble. The view of creamy flesh was exquisite. "What about thieves, robbers and that lot?"

Her chin rose an inch. "Them, too."

"Wonderful. I feel safer already." He smiled at her blatantly. It was obvious she was lying through her teeth.

"If your smile is meant as subterfuge, it's not working," she said, realizing he'd called her bluff. "Actually, we haven't had any thieves, robbers and that sort up here lately. Well . . . ever, actually."

"Oh? Mind if I ask why you circled behind me instead of coming up the road?"

"I was keeping an eye out for wild grapevines. I harvest and sell them to craft shops."

"Do you now?"

Kaley was becoming irritated with herself because she couldn't seem to do the appropriate thing, which was retreat. But Poseidon didn't seem inclined to bring their meeting to a halt, either. It was as if a magnet hindered their movement, keeping them both locked inside its pull.

"You're not from around here," she snapped, "or you'd know the courteous thing to do is ask permission to make camp."

"Now, missy, a man doesn't need permission to take up residence on his own land."

"This is private property. You're trespassing. Camping for a few days—fine, but we don't tolerate squatters."

"I can appreciate that," he said agreeably. "Truth of it, I'd be happy to have you to supper one evening—after we've settled in and put the roof on the old place." He gestured behind him toward a copse of trees. "Oops."

He repositioned the hat over his abdomen.

"You're getting me stirred up, missy. I can't think straight. Forgot my manners entirely. Name's Slater Rutledge. Lately of Andamooka, Australia, but more recently, Atlanta, Georgia. I was born on this mountain."

Australia? She glanced at the tattoos on his biceps. One was the head, hooves and flying mane of a wild stallion. Probably apt, she thought. The other looked like a kangaroo. It was a kangaroo. She repeated his name to herself. He was born on Crosswind? Clarity struck. She stared at him blankly. "You're a *Rutledge?*"

"And you'd be one of the Jackson clan."

"Yes... but you could've read that on the mailbox!" He couldn't be a Rutledge! Let him be anybody but a Rutledge!

"Matter-of-factly, I did. Now, missy, I like the idea of you standing there admiring me, but I've got a bath to finish and a roof to build."

"But—you can't have come back to the mountain. You killed Independent's wife and daughter-in-law!"

"Not me, missy. I've never laid a hand on a woman outside a bedroom."

"I don't mean you personally," she admitted. "You're too young to have been involved. But that won't make one whit of difference to Independent. You're a Rutledge."

His eyes narrowed, losing their hypnotic gaze. "Far as I know, no Rutledge was ever hanged for murder. The talk in my family was that there was an accident, and that was thirty years ago."

"Thirty years doesn't mean spit to Independent! He's never stopped mourning."

"I do admire loyalty and dedication. After my daddy died, my momma set his plate at the table for every meal. Never did get to sit in his chair. Always wanted to, though, just to see how a dead man ate."

Kaley glared at Slater Rutledge, shunting aside the pleasant sound of his whiskey-and-tobacco drawl, the angular face that had an odd sort of appeal, the inviting eyes and the rest of him that was so magnificently male. "You can't be serious about living up here."

"Am."

"But—" Kaley stopped. The fallow field behind the tumbledown Rutledge homestead had been her best source of baby's breath and walking fern. Her thoughts went into a spin, fathoming the implication of a Rutledge returning to Crosswind Mountain. If she didn't handle this right, she'd be out of business within six weeks!

"I'm Kaley Jackson." It was some foolish part of herself that added, "Virgil Jackson's widow."

Slater digested the information. He looked at her throat, slender and tanned; at her chest that rose and fell. Ah, now. She was making it too easy. Into a small pool of silence, he said, "Pleased to make your acquaintance, Kaley. Now, if you'll excuse me . . ."

A cool polite statement, lacking future promise. Kaley was nonplussed. "I—of course."

"I don't mind if you want to cut across the creek and take the short route home."

"I would, but as I said, I'm scouting gravevines."

"Begging your pardon—not on Rutledge land and not without my permission."

"Your permission! This land has been abandoned for thirty years! I've established the right to use it."

He dipped his head slightly. The sun bounced off his gleaming hair. "Let's just say you were borrowing the use of Rutledge land, seeing as how there wasn't a Rutledge on hand to look after it."

"I'll pay you to let me harvest grapevines and shrubs."

"I appreciate the offer, but I don't like doing business with my boots off."

Kaley brightened. "I'll turn my back while you get dressed."

"There's another thing, missy. I don't like being hurried."

Kaley bit back a scathing retort. She was fed up with him calling her missy. "I understand," she said coolly. "But will you *discuss* the possibility?"

"Glad to."

His answer was ambiguous. Kaley understood it was the only one she'd get, today anyway.

She dredged up a smile that to Slater looked like the rictus of a mouse snatched from its nest by a hawk. He also noted, half grimace or not, it didn't detract from her looks.

"I'll let you get back to your bath, Mr. Rutledge. You must be freezing. That stream is as cold as the Arctic."

"I'm warm as toast, missy, but thanks for the thought." He was chilled through. He'd been standing still so long minnows were beginning to nibble on his toes. Still, the discomfort was worth it. He couldn't have conjured up a sheila as interesting of face, as substantial of curves, or as spicy of tongue had he been ordered to do so at the point of a gun.

Kaley paused. "Mr. Rutledge—"

"Make it Slater. We're neighbors."

"Perhaps you and your family would come to supper at our place. Instead of driving past the switchback, you turn onto it. You'll pass a pumpkin field then a cornfield, plowed under. Just follow the lane on past the stand of walnut trees."

"That's a kindly offer."

"You'll come? Tomorrow, perhaps?"

"Have to give it some thought." Lots of thought. The main one being how to go calling without Lacy and Jason tagging along.

"I don't suppose you have a telephone yet?"

Slater sighed. The trappings of civilization. He supposed he'd have to investigate the possibility. "Not yet."

"Well, just come. We don't put on airs." She began making her way up the incline, but her mind wasn't on sharp stones and slippery footholds. It was roiling with how to tell Independent she'd invited a Rutledge to supper, and how to convince him why it was necessary.

Lips pursed in thought, Slater tracked Kaley with his eyes. The dangling blue ribbon caught on a bush as she leaned forward to balance herself. He opened his mouth to alert her, but he changed his mind.

At the top of the slate run Kaley slipped behind a tree.

She knew it was out-and-out voyeurism, but except for a museum, it was unlikely she would ever again see such a magnificent specimen of a man in the nude, however much a hardhead he meant to be about the grapevines.

Slater Rutledge was again immersed in the icy stream, his cigar in his mouth, his hat on his head. He looked for all the world as if he were soaking in a steaming Roman bath.

Then she saw that neither her stealth nor her gaze had escaped his keen eyes.

He was tipping his hat respectfully.

Caught, yet certain he couldn't see thc mortification in her cheeks, Kaley felt obliged to wave.

"Neanderthal," she muttered.

"Hell of a sheila," Slater said.

He frowned as he felt a quick stab of pressure building behind his eyes.

Silently cursing the fates that had dropped the sword of Damocles on him when he was least expecting it, he sidled toward the bank of the stream and donned his clothes.

Chapter Two

"How can we live here?" ten-year-old Lacy exclaimed, her wizened, inelegant little face reflecting the artless, unadulterated scorn she reserved for grown-ups. "There're hardly any walls! The roof is falling in. What're we gonna cook on? And we're not goin' to take a bath in a creek. It's unsanitary!"

"Listen, you half-pint jilleroo," Slater said, longing for somewhere to curl up and massage his temples until the pain went away. "Cut the sass and help unload the truck. Neither of you wanted a bath after the long trip, so you must be ready to work. Take old Helpless with you." He waved a callused hand, indicating her brother.

"I won't! This place is gross. It's full of bugs and spiders!"

"Bloody hell, missy! I've survived snakebite, flood, drought, quicksand and mine cave-ins. But all of that pales in comparison to being stuck with you, and... and..."

"Jason," Lacy supplied, leading her argument with her chin while draping an arm around her five-year-old brother. "You might have lived in dumpy places in

Australia, but this is the United States. To ask little kids like us to live here is child abuse!"

"Why, you insufferable little—"

"And don't call Jason helpless. He's just delicate." She sniffed, posturing fearlessness, and added a dig of her own. "Your left foot is bigger than he was when he was born."

Slater glared at the girl and pushed back his hat, unconsciously fingering the brim. "I top out at six foot three, missy. Now wouldn't I just look funny prancing about on size nines?"

"You look funny anyway. Your hair is almost as long as mine."

"Never mind my looks. We're stuck with each other until Aunt Willie gets out of the hospital. I don't like it any more than you do. Now, get your swag from the truck. It won't take much to put this place in order—a few nails, some roofing, a broom—" He eyed the great old stacked-stone fireplace. Cleaning the chimney of sparrow nests and bat droppings was what had sent him into the creek. "I'll get a fire going and we can roast some hot dogs."

"I gotta go to the bathroom," announced Jason.

Slater pointed toward the threshold with his cigar. The door was sagging and draped with spiderwebs, which caught the last feeble rays of sun. "Pick any tree, but get some distance from the house."

Lucy gasped. "You mean we're supposed to go to the toilet in the *woods?*"

"I hardly think there's anything in the wilds of Tennessee that'll jump up and bite you on your arse."

"Just because you're bigger doesn't mean you can bully us. Wait until our mother gets here."

Slater snorted. Based on what he'd learned from Aunt Willie, the woman didn't deserve the title. On the other hand, if the broad did show up, maybe she'd take these two off his hands. "Really, missy? You expecting her?"

"Aunt Willie sent her a letter when Daddy died. She'll come for us. I know she will. And when she does . . ."

The childish threat trailed. Slater rubbed his temple. "Can't be too soon for me, missy. Now, get on outside and do your business. You can wash up out of a bucket. We'll eat, and then bed down."

"Where?"

"We'll put our swag down in front of the fireplace."

"On the floor? You expect us to sleep on the floor? No way!"

"Lacy Rutledge, you've got a problem with your mouth. You wanna sleep on a nice soft bed, conjure one up!"

"I want my daddy," Jason said, his eyes beginning to well with tears.

"Daddy's in heaven," Lacy said, leading him out of the house, stopping long enough to mug Slater a perverse look over her shoulder.

He recognized her expression was just for good measure, equal to getting in the last word. He had never in his life hit a woman or child. Clenching his jaw, he surmised it wouldn't take long for the girl to bullyrag that principle to shreds.

"Then I want to go to heaven, too," Jason cried.

"Don't we all," Slater muttered morosely.

Truth to tell, if he held up his homecoming to the cold light of logic, he'd be crying, too.

The pain behind his eyes was growing worse.

Bloody doctors. All they'd done was count out pills and recommend him to avoid stress. Cripes almighty! He could figure that one out for himself. Be damned if he'd take any of the medicine the doctors had pressed on him. Considering the lot he'd drawn, he needed his wits about him.

As of seventy-two hours ago and by virtue of his brother's death, he had been declared de facto head of the family, made the reluctant keeper of his niece and nephew, and given the charge of rebuilding the old family homestead to its former glory. The unfairness of it all made him yearn for the two-room shack he'd called home in the sweltering opal fields of Andamooka.

He'd planned on coming home with a bang, dangling his cache of opals and gold under the nose of his upright, superior-acting older brother who, since childhood, had smirked at Slater's every endeavor.

Instead he'd arrived stateside in time for his brother's sudden death. To add insult to injury, he'd had to pay the mortician.

Good old Jerome's real estate empire had collapsed in on him. To hear Aunt Willie tell it, the only thing keeping Jerome upright since his wife left him had been "Rutledge pride, a stiff upper lip and the starch in his shirts."

Aunt Willie was another shock. The keeper of family lore and secrets had become frail in the ten years he'd spent roaming Australia. Hurrying to catch up to Jason at the funeral, she'd stumbled over a gravestone and broken her leg. After the ambulance had taken her to the hospital, he'd found himself corralled in her tiny apartment and responsible for Jerome's two sprouts.

He couldn't say what had made him hang around long enough for Aunt Willie to start issuing orders. Confusion, perhaps.

Moreover, here he was executing her instructions, down to "be kind to the children."

If ever a man had gone from sitting in the lap of the gods to being booted in the butt, it was himself. Disgusted, he tossed his cigar into the stone hearth and bent down to fire the kindling.

While the wood caught, the chill of night settled over the mountain. Owls hooted. Down by the creek an occasional frog croaked a throaty note or two.

Slater hauled out the things he judged they'd need for the night. He wished he'd thought to sink a six-pack into the stream. A cool beer would go down nicely before he tucked in.

Inside, they built a fire in the fireplace. He roasted the hot dogs on sticks, dipped them into mustard and passed them to the kids who washed them down with tin cups of water hauled from the creek.

"Uncle Slater?" Jason said, his voice slightly quivery. "Are you gonna keep the fire goin' all night?"

Slater looked at the boy. Fear was in his face though he was trying hard not to show it. Recalling how he'd felt when his own parents had died took the edge off Slater's voice. "Planned on it. Unless you'd rather not."

"Oh, no. I *like* the fire. It dances." Still, he inched closer to his sister and gazed out the open door to shadows growing long and into eerie shapes.

Slater sighed inwardly, knowing instinctively he had to do something to take the kids' minds off their predicament. "You want to see fire that can really dance?" he said, and was rewarded by both children looking at him curiously.

He rummaged into his canvas swag and pulled out a small wooden chest. From inside it he withdrew a worn chamois bag and spread its contents out on the floor. "Opals and gold nuggets," he told. "Go on, you can touch them. Hold 'em up so they catch the light."

He tensed as the kids gleefully sorted and handled the gemstones as if they were marbles. Bloody hell! He couldn't believe he was allowing a couple of pint-size jackaroos to play with upwards a hundred thousand dollars' worth of gemstones. On the other hand, the damned things might as well *be* marbles for all the satisfaction they'd brought him.

Holding an opal up to the light of the fire, Lacy asked him, "What's a jilleroo?"

"In your case, it'd be a female station hand. She helps round up and break wild horses."

Lacy picked up another opal. "Aunt Willie says you're wild."

"That so? Perhaps she's right. I don't take to backfillin' and breakin' as easy as some."

Lacy gathered up the opals and nuggets and handed them back to Slater as if returning a bribe not up to her standards. "I don't understand why we couldn't stay at Aunt Willie's instead of coming here."

"This is home, missy. Get used to it. Now crawl into your swags and go to sleep. We have a hard day ahead of us tomorrow."

He lifted himself off the floor and went onto the porch to have a smoke.

The lonely rustle of the cool night wind felt good on his brow. The eaves on the old house creaked, a melancholy sound.

Savoring the taste of fine tobacco, he closed his eyes. A picture of Kaley Jackson flitted across his mind's eye and he smiled. It was her eyes that made her face what it was. Luminous and thickly lashed, he'd bet his best opal that she never bothered with female paint.

He opened his eyes to erase the vision.

If he'd ever needed proof that fate was coated with irony, he had only to point to the likes of Kaley Jackson.

At the very point in his life when he had no use for a woman, no time to pursue her, and no future to offer even if he did, one comes tumbling down a mountainside almost into his lap.

Still, there was no harm in accepting her invitation to supper. Or spending a few pleasant minutes recalling the rise and fall of her breasts and the firm backside she presented when she started back up the slate run. He felt a pinprick of desire working its way into his groin.

But even while he allowed himself to be swept up into the moment, his head throbbed, reminding him that discovering the cause of his headaches had been another kick in the gut.

He decided not to look too far ahead to the pitfalls, regardless of how obvious and deep.

He ground out the cigar stub beneath his heel and stretched. In the house Lacy and Jason had curled up together in a single sleeping bag.

He smoothed out his own kit and lay atop it, elbow crooked behind his head as he gazed into the fire. Kaley Jackson appeared in the flames. The vision of her body went right to his nerves, and his hands nearly reached out to her.

"Bloody hell!"

He turned away from the fire and fell into a restless sleep.

"I CAN'T BELIEVE you did something so stupid," Jessie said as she rummaged through her nurse's bag. "He could've been a deer poacher. Or a moonshiner cooking down whiskey. It's the time of year for it. Corn's been harvested. As soon as you spied his smoke, you should've called the sheriff. Now, come away from that sink and let me tend those elbows."

"My elbows are fine." Kaley sat at the table anyway and allowed Jessie to minister to her. "The man's a lech. A sexual corsair."

"Oh?" Jessie's eyebrows shot up. "Sounds like my kind of man." She dabbed on antiseptic. Kaley yelped.

"No wonder Independent runs and hides when you show up."

Jessie laughed. "Be nice."

"I don't feel like being nice. How am I going to make a living if I can't harvest Rutledge land?"

"Get a job in Jamestown?"

Kaley pursed her lips as she moved back to the sink. "Very funny. I couldn't survive a nine-to-five job. Neither could you."

Jessie closed her bag with a snap. "You're het up, my friend. It looks good on you. Your cheeks are flushed, your eyes are shining. I bet your blood is running a little hot, too, isn't it?"

Kaley cocked her chin Jessie's way. "Tell you what," she said, "come to supper tomorrow night and meet him. I could use some moral support with Independent anyway. He's death on Rutledges."

"You're taking advantage of my being a nurse. I don't like the sight of blood any more than the next person. I have enough trouble trying to catch up with that old goat just to give him his cortisone shots. What do you expect me to do? Step in the line of fire?"

"Actually, yes," Kaley said, smiling to deflect the truth of her words, the line of fire she had in mind being more between herself and Slater Rutledge rather than Slater and Independent. "I'd do the same for you."

"It must be the altitude," Jessie complained. "You're becoming as crazy and stubborn as the rest of the natives. Why do the dumb thing and invite a Rutledge to supper when you knew there was a feud between the families? Did the guy look like he was starving?"

"Feud? Jessie, that happened thirty years ago! Independent is mostly bluff."

"I beg to differ with you. Independent *did* shoot the drunk who drove into the yard and ran over Sarah and Lou Ann. And the man was drunk because Hiram Rutledge sold him raw whiskey."

"Everybody in Fentress County knows that old story, Jessie. The drunk slammed into that old walnut tree by the well. He was already dead when Independent blasted him. Anyway Rutledge looks like he can take care of himself."

"Oh?" Jessie arched an eyebrow. "How else did he look?"

Strong. Sexy. Commanding. "Like a man," Kaley said loftily. "You know what men look like."

"There're men and then there're men. Which is our Mr. Rutledge?"

"Married, apparently."

"I see. So the impression you're trying to make is on his wife?"

"I'm not trying to make an impression on anybody."

Jessie flicked her wrist, dismissing Kaley's explanation out of hand.

"Well, just for the record, I wouldn't let you within a mile of any man I was interested in."

"I don't put myself in the path of men," Kaley bristled. "Especially not married men."

Yet, she had not been able to shake from her mind the converging planes of Rutledge's face, the unexpected dimples, the powerhouse of rippling masculine muscles. Just thinking of the man put her off center.

"Admit it, you're ripe for a relationship."

"This is a disgusting conversation."

"No, it isn't."

Kaley chewed the inside of her lip. She wanted to admit the attraction she felt for Slater Rutledge. She had never thought it would happen, but time's calendar had offset the memories of Virgil. There would always be a special, tucked-away place in her heart for him—but he wasn't *here.* Slater Rutledge was vibrant, electric and alive.

"They may not come," she said finally. "Rutledge didn't exactly say yes."

"Did he exactly say no?"

Kaley shook her head.

Jessie rolled her eyes. "Did he exactly say he was married and going to bring *Mrs.* Rutledge?"

Kaley's heart stopped for an instant. "No."

I'd be happy to have you to supper one evening—after we've settled in and put up the roof.

That was married, wasn't it?

"And he was just wading in the creek?"

"Rinsing out a cloth or something."

"Washing his clothes by flaying them on rocks, I'll warrant. Where was this wife of his? Grubbing in the fields?"

"Jessie, either you're coming tomorrow night or you're not. Which is it?"

"I've never met anyone who's lived in Australia, swum with sharks, wrestled crocs—"

Kaley sighed. "I didn't say he was Crocodile Dundee. All I want to do is make for a pleasant evening. I can't take no for an answer. He *has* to let me harvest Rutledge land. I'd never be able to stay here working for minimum wage. Part of the reason Independent tolerates me is that I can take care of myself."

"What're some of the other reasons?"

Kaley laughed. "I aggravate him. He loves aggravation." She sobered. "I have barely enough stock to see me through Thanksgiving orders. My standing Christmas orders are what get me through the year, and the money from the new orders, well, I was going to build some more drying sheds."

"Then if you're not the least bit worried, why do you need moral support?"

"Dammit! Will you come or not?"

"Am I coming as guest, family friend or county nurse?"

"Whichever you prefer."

"Okay. Guest. That way even if I have to sew up battle wounds, I won't be expected to help with dishes afterward."

Kaley hugged her friend then linked her arm in Jessie's and led her outside into the dusk. "You are a true friend."

"I'm aware of that. Who else could you get to listen to you rant on and on about this grand new neighbor of yours?"

"I'm making baked Alaska for dessert tomorrow, Jessie. *Yours* is going to be laced with arsenic."

The nurse chuckled. "Well, dearie, a little arsenic has always been good for the complexion. Staves off the ravages of age."

As they stepped into the yard, they both looked toward the crest of Crosswind Mountain. "I wonder if he plans to farm or what. That spine up there is so steep, roots have to grab on to a rock to keep from sliding down into the ravine."

"Maybe he just wants the peace and quiet."

Kaley shook her head. "He's not the type."

Jessie gave a half smile. "I'll take your word for it. Tell Independent I stopped in."

"I don't have to. He knows you're here. He's probably sitting up there in his pumpkin field waiting until he hears your car drive off."

Jessie Lukazewski made a sound of derision. "All the jokes about us Poles aside, we're a determined, patient lot. I'm going to administer that damned shot of cortisone to his old crippled hip even if I have to do it on his deathbed." Thoughtful, she turned toward the Jackson family cemetery that stood two dozen yards away on a small hillock.

Unfenced, it was filled with the leafy shadow of walnut trees and the bygone dreams and hopes of those left behind.

Kaley followed her gaze. "Sometimes it's hard to believe I've been here five years," she said softly. "And in spite of... everything, it's been good. If I regret anything, it's only that Virgil and I didn't have a baby. I'd have liked that."

"Don't go melancholy on me," Jessie said.

"I'm not."

Kaley drew her gaze back from the graveyard, and met her own reflection in the polished window of Jessie's car. She saw a woman in her late twenties wearing a plaid cotton shirt, open at the throat to reveal a slender tanned neck; the woman's hair was dark, shoulder-length and wavy, brushed back from her oval face. The fingers of her hands were sturdy and short-nailed. Though she wasn't vain, Kaley knew she had an attractive face, yet nothing in the image hinted at the emotional pain she'd suffered.

"I do get angry sometimes, Jessie. Not at Virgil anymore for dying, but at myself. I didn't insist we have a child."

"Fate stepped in is all. You've got to remember things happen for a reason."

"No good reason that I can name. I could've taken care of a baby and still run the business."

"Don't beat up on yourself with hindsight. Your goal was to learn the business, get it off the ground so you and Virgil could work it together. I wish I had the luxury of your convenient memory lapses. You spent the first eight months here helping Independent get back on his feet—"

"For which he has never forgiven me."

Jessie laughed. "You bathed him every day. That's too citified and humiliating for his kind. Once a week is plenty. I suspect some of Independent's intolerance comes from the fact that Virgil was his only grandchild. He raised him up in mountain ways and what did Virgil do? Why he slipped his traces and went off to collect an elegant wife with all these highfalutin ideas."

"Elegant!" Kaley laughed. "I haven't worn a pair of high heels since I set foot on this farm. All I did was clean up this place!"

"It was Independent's dirt."

"Well, he's got all the dirt he can use out in that shack he huddles in. He won't let me near it."

"Speaking of not coming near, have you heard from your parents lately?"

The sparkle in Kaley's luminous gray eyes dulled for a moment. "No, and it's just as well. They're never going to accept that I *like* my life-style."

"Hope for the best. They'll come around eventually." Jessie glanced at her watch. "I can't linger another second. I've an entire week of charts and logs to finish up." The friends hugged, and Jessie left with a promise to return for dinner the next night.

From the pumpkin field in the distance, Kaley could hear Independent's old mule braying. "Sounds like Flossie knows it's her dinnertime even if Independent doesn't." With that, she decided to take a walk up the switchback to check up on the old codger and break the news about a Rutledge coming to dinner.

FOR ONE BRIEF INSTANT Independent gaped at Kaley from across Flossie's shoulders. "You can't have gone and done a fool thing like ask a Rutledge to sit to my table!"

She eyed the old man with despair. He was livid, his wrinkled face sharp with an age-old pain, his hand on the mule's cropped mane was palsied with anger. Even his bushy gray eyebrows quivered. She spoke harshly, trying not to sound as if she was addressing a child. "It won't hurt to have them to supper just once."

His face filled with disgust. "If a Rutledge sets foot on Jackson land, I'll shoot him. Rutledges killed my wife and Virgil's mother. Don't that stick in your craw?"

Kaley inhaled. "I'm sad that it happened, but Slater Rugledge didn't do it. He couldn't have been more than a toddler."

"It don't make no nevermind. The happiest day of my life was when that clan hightailed it off this mountain. I went down to the switchback and watched them depart. I held my rifle sights then because there was women and children ridin' in the back of the trucks, else—"

Kaley tried another tack. "If I'm to stay in business, I *have* to be able to harvest Rutledge land."

"That don't make no nevermind to me. You don't belong here anyways. Virgil wasn't thinkin' straight when he brung you here. Now he's gone, you orta just go home to your ma an' leave an old man in peace."

"If I wasn't here to take care of you, you'd die."

Independent snorted. "I'd die happy. But before I did, I'd burn all that froufrou you got scattered in the place. It ain't fittin' a man don't recognize the house he was raised up in."

"If that's how you feel, burn it now! And if you want to murder and maim the Rutledges, do! That'd sure take care of my problem. They'd be dead, and you'd be in jail. I'd have the whole mountain to myself."

Independent bared his teeth. "Heh? Gave away your strategy, ain't you? Don't expect me to oblige you so wholesomely. Now git away from me and my mule. You ain't fit company."

Sighing heavily, Kaley dropped back. Flossie flattened her ears, bared her teeth, stretched her neck and tried to bite her. Kaley squealed and sidestepped out of reach.

"Good mule!" Independent cackled, his laughter reverberating down the switchback.

She spun around. "The Rutledges are coming to supper, old man, and you better behave yourself."

Still grinning, Independent shook his hoe at her. "Scat! Afore I sic my mule on ye!"

Chapter Three

Out of long habit, Slater was awake and out-of-doors at the first hint of dawn. He rummaged in the old lean-to next to the barn for an ax. He found three. The one with the sturdiest handle had the dullest edge, but it would do for splitting logs into firewood.

He scouted the woods nearby the homestead until he found a walnut tree brought down long ago by a bolt of lightning. It lay across a deer path. He could see where their delicate hooves bit into the soft earth in preparation for the leap over the obstruction.

Within ten minutes he had the rhythm: brace the legs, swing the ax, feel the head bite into the wood, jiggle the blade, withdraw; brace and swing again.

The sun rose higher. Sweat gathered in his armpits and beaded on his brow. Stopping for a moment, he brushed the sweat away with the back of his hand. Taking up the ax again, he briefly scanned the forest, disbelieving his eyes when he saw Kaley Jackson moving toward him on the narrow deer path. He rested the ax handle against his thigh.

"Well, well, well," he said softly. "If it isn't the widow Jackson, come to call." He watched her approach, appreciative of the way she filled out the soft cotton shirt. Her hair was pulled back so that her eyes betrayed a vibrancy. He was just cocksure enough to take credit for that shine.

"I hope you don't mind," she said hesitantly, halting a yard or so away. "I heard the ax." She'd more than heard it. The sound reverberating down the mountainside had been like a beacon she couldn't resist.

"I'd ask you in for a cuppa," he said, nodding toward the homestead in the distance, "but we're not really set up for company."

"Oh, no thanks." She didn't yet want to come face-to-face with his family and destroy the fantasies she'd spent the night weaving around him. Looking down on Slater from the slate run yesterday, he had seemed a large man; being on the same level with him now gave her a greater appreciation of his size. He was every bit as magnificent and overwhelming with his clothes on as off.

He wore soft khaki pants tucked into much-worn and scuffed hide boots. The sleeves of his blue work shirt had been ripped out, showing biceps gleaming with sweat that highlighted the tattoos. Against his thigh, the ax handle appeared little more than a loosely held twig.

"You're just out for a morning stroll?"

"No. I really wasn't very nice yesterday. I just wanted to welcome you to Crosswind and confirm that you and your family are coming to supper tonight."

"Well, thanks, missy. And, I'm still considering it."

"My grandfather-in-law isn't too happy that I've asked you."

His smile arched icily. "You're withdrawing the invitation?" He felt a keen sense of disappointment.

"Oh, no. *I* want you to come. It's just...Independent won't...I don't want you to be offended, but he probably won't be joining us. He's as stubborn as his old mule."

Slater's eyes narrowed. This was a horse of a different color. "Spit it out, missy. Are you suggesting I might be bushwhacked?"

"Of course not! Independent does more posturing than anything else. But he can be verbally unpleasant. I wouldn't want you to think I agree with him."

"About what?"

"The past. The grudge between your families."

He digested this with a murmur. "There's no grudge on my part, missy. At least not against a Jackson."

"So, you'll come?"

"I have to see how the day goes." He had every intention of accepting her invitation, but only at the last minute, lest he had one of his damnable headaches and not be fit company for a snake.

"I'll check with you later in the day," she said hopefully.

"Fine." He picked up the ax and tested its balance, seeming anxious to get back to work.

"Later, then," Kaley said, knowing she'd been dismissed. She moved back down the path accompanied by the rhythm of the ax biting into wood.

Slater finished splitting the firewood and gathered up a hefty armload. He dumped it on the floor in the kitchen, waking up Lacy and Jason with the clatter. He ordered them up, and while they took themselves off to the creek for a bucket of water, he cleaned the soot out from the draw pipes of the old cookstove. By the time they returned to the house, he had pork and beans bubbling in a pan.

The bucket they brought back held barely two cups of water. "Cripes almighty! That won't go around a corner."

Lacy sniffed. "It got heavy. We had to pour some out." Dour-faced, she eyed the beans. "You don't expect us to eat canned beans for breakfast?"

"I want Coco Puffs and milk," announced Jason.

Slater spooned the beans onto tin camp plates and banged them on the dusty table. "Eat or starve. We have work to do."

Lacy balked. "Not us. We have to go to school. We have our report cards and transfer papers. You have to take us to register. After that, we'll ride the school bus. Aunt Willie said."

Slater snorted. "Aunt Willie said! I'm sick of hearing 'Aunt Willie said.' I'd like to wring that old crone's neck."

"Better not. Then you'd be stuck with us for sure. At least until our momma gets here," she added, refusing to give up.

"You can go to school next week."

He waited for a tin cup of water to boil, then stirred coffee grounds into it and waited for them to settle.

"The law'll get you if you don't take us to school," Lacy insisted around a mouthful of beans.

"Don't talk with your mouth full!"

She spit the beans out. "Okay."

"Why you little tree devil. Clean that up!"

The girl glared at him, her brow furrowed. Her expression was all Rutledge, stubborn and dug in.

"All right, missy," he said, barely civil. "Get yourselves cleaned up. Better to have you in school all day than traipsing at my heels like store-bought puppies. I can use the space."

"You mean outta sight, outta mind, don't you?"

"Same thing."

"We'll need money for lunch and pencils and paper."

"I didn't take you to raise."

"Momma will pay you back when she gets here."

Slater poured his coffee, blew on it and took a test sip. He had it in mind to tell the chit her mother was never going to show, but Aunt Willie had cautioned him on that.

"The child has to have something to cling to, Slater. Her world has collapsed. Just ignore it when she makes claims about her mother. Renie has shown up one Christmas out of four and been months late on birthdays. You won't have to worry with Jason as far as Renie is concerned, he doesn't remember her. He was just a bit of a thing when she took off. Just you go on up to the old place and get it ready. Soon's I'm up, I'll join you and help with the kids till you take a wife."

"Plan on dying on the homestead, then," he told her heatedly. "I'm not tying myself down to a sheila, or two brats spurned by their own mother."

Aunt Willie'd eyed him from the cranked-up hospital bed. "Slater, you can't fault children for the parents' sway. They've never done you any harm. And neither have I. Keep up that talk and I'll send the nurse to find me a switch and tan your backside like I used to."

He'd laughed then. Aunt Willie had shrunk to five feet of brittle bone and two yards of desiccated skin.

"What's funny?" Lacy asked, shaking him from the reverie.

"Nothing." He spied a bit of blue in her hair. So that's where Kaley's ribbon had got to. The girl had snitched it. "Take that ribbon out of your hair. It's not yours."

Lacy skipped out of his reach. "It is now. I found it."

Two strides and he had her pinned. He yanked the ribbon loose and put it in his pocket.

"Leave my sister alone!" Jason cried, throwing himself at Slater's legs.

Slater tried shaking the boy off. "Hey! Stop that." He felt sharp little teeth sinking into his thigh. "Cripes almighty!"

Lacy tugged on Jason and pulled him loose. "I hate you, Uncle Slater! You mean old thing. I saw you naked with that woman. I know what you were gonna do. You're a womanizer. Aunt Willie said!"

Slater turned to the boy. "Fetch me a switch and be quick about it."

"If you hit us, I'll tell the teacher," Lacy warned.

"Get in the truck," Slater roared, smarting with agitation. "And one more remark will see you plunked on the side of the highway to find your own way to school.''

''We could do that,'' Lacy vowed, unbowed. ''We're Rutledges.''

''You can't be,'' he shot back. ''A Rutledge doesn't spy on his kin.''

''I wasn't looking on purpose! And I oughta be able to keep the ribbon. Finders keepers!''

''Wrong, missy. We know the owner. It has to be returned.''

Lacy sniffed. ''Won't do you any good. She don't like you, either.''

''Sure, she does.''

''No, she doesn't. She called you a name. I heard her.''

Slater frowned. ''What kind of name?''

''A bad one.''

''What?''

''I can't tell you. I don't say bad words. And anyway, I forgot.''

He scowled. ''Hint at it.''

''I can't think on an empty stomach. Maybe if you buy us a hamburger on the way to school, it'll come to me.''

An hour and twenty minutes later as the children were being led down the hall by their respective teachers, Lacy turned back to her uncle. ''Neanderthal,'' she said, grinning.

The surprised teacher looked back at him and dispensed a scowl of disapproval.

Forcing a smile, he touched his hat brim. ''Family joke, ma'am.''

On his way out of the school, Slater decided Lacy was going to be the first of the Rutledges to be skinned, gutted, and hung up to dry.

KALEY WAS SO DISTRACTED at the grocery store that she had to keep checking and rechecking her grocery list.

It was true that she did not put herself in the path of men. Until today. And she'd done it deliberately.

Usually she worked until she dropped, and ignored the sensual demands of her body. But recalling Slater's broad chest, powerful thighs, and the way his mouth shaped words, brought out feelings in her that she kept suppressed, feelings that made her think of making love.

Dear God, but she missed sex.

And Slater Rutledge looked like a man who knew how to please a woman.

She ordered the butcher to cut her a ten-pound standing-rib roast.

The butcher stared at the woman who had once returned nine ounces of raw fat from a lamb roast and asked for a refund.

He gave Kaley a wintry smile. "It's three dollars and seventy-nine cents a pound."

"Wrap it."

I've lost my mind, she thought.

It was only that Slater Rutledge was a big man and no doubt had an appetite to match. She wondered about the extent of all his other appetites.

There was no emotional room for a married man in her life.

He would never know how attracted she was to him.

They could be friends. Business partners.

As she pulled out of the parking lot there came a squeal of brakes and a frantic honking. She looked over her shoulder to find the front grille of Miss Broom's ancient maroon Packard a foot from her nose. Miss Broom was hunched down behind the steering column, her face petrified in fear.

Kaley made exaggerated motions of apology and backed up into the parking lot.

The Packard followed and parked alongside.

Kaley groaned. She was in for a lecture on the carelessness and omissions of the young, one of the elderly teacher's favorite topics.

She was going to have to eat humble pie and pretend she liked it. Moreover, in this instance, it was well deserved.

She got out of her car and went around to face Miss Broom, who by now was standing beside the fender, smoothing out her gray skirt. The elderly woman always dressed in gray print dresses, lace collars and old-fashioned black, lace-up shoes that could still be had at Wright's general store. Miss Broom had been girlhood friends with Independent's wife, Sarah, and had taught Virgil's dad, Ethan, and Virgil himself, in the fourth grade.

She looked up as Kaley approached. "Well, my dear, you almost put 'paid' to the next ten years I have coming, not to mention snuffing out the lives of the two youngsters I have in hand."

Kaley dipped her head and looked into the back seat of the Packard. A boy and a girl sat there, stiff as boards, faces bereft of expression. "Miss Broom, I'm terribly sorry, my mind was elsewhere."

"No doubt you've been sipping Independent Jackson's brew and it's addled your brain."

Miss Broom occasionally appeared at the farm to reminisce old times in Fentress County with Independent. Kaley suspected the teacher was sweet on her grandfather-in-law. "I haven't been drinking, Miss Broom. I was daydreaming."

"No concentration, that's the fault with you young people. But lucky you, Kaley Jackson, I'm going to give you the opportunity to make amends." Miss Broom signaled to the two children to get out of her car. "You can take these two on along home. They went and missed their school bus." She frowned a remonstrance at the girl of about ten. "This one got into a scrap. On what account I can't say. She's clammed up tighter than a hamstrung mule."

"But—" Kaley began, looking from the children to Miss Broom to the bags of food in the back of her pickup. "I'm really pushed for time."

"It won't be out of your way, and it's a neighborly thing to do. I'm sure they know their way from your place to theirs. They'd have to walk past it to get down to the bus stop of a morning anyway."

"They would?"

Miss Broom smiled cannily. "They're Rutledges. I imagine that's giving Independent fits. That old riffraff never did like competition."

The Rutledge name brought Kaley up sharply.

"Rutledge? Why, I've met their father."

Miss Broom lowered her voice an octave. "You haven't—not unless you've visited heaven or hell recently. They're wards of their uncle—Slater Rutledge. What a sad lot that bodes for them is beyond thought. I haven't heard from Wilhemina Rutledge in years—the poor dear was his aunt and has probably passed on—but I can tell you she was highly displeased with Slater. Highly displeased," she repeated knowingly. "A scoundrel and a drifter, she named him. Not that she came right out and said as much, but reading between the lines..."

Kaley digested that tidbit of information. Her mind was suddenly a blurred kaleidoscope of light and movement. "Perhaps he's settled down some. He has a wife, doesn't he?" Her voice sounded strained and nervous.

Shaking her head, Miss Broom continued in a stage whisper. "No, and more's the pity. From what her homeroom teacher told me, that girl could do with a bit of mothering."

Kaley needed desperately to have it spelled out. "You're certain Slater Rutledge isn't married?"

"Of course I'm certain. The principal invited him and his wife to attend the PTA. He told her there wasn't a missus and he didn't have the time. And that's a shame, too. Would've been nice for you to have womenfolk near about." She patted Kaley's arm. "It's too lonely up there for you."

Kaley's heart and head were pounding in different rhythms. "It's not lonely. Independent keeps me company."

Miss Broom snorted delicately. "I know better than that. He keeps company with his mule and a jug, and not necessarily in that order. Tell him I said hello and—"

Kaley had an idea. "Why don't you tell him yourself, Miss Broom. Come to dinner tonight. Jessie will be there and the Rutledges are invited—"

Miss Broom expressed shock. "Independent agreed to sit to table with the Rutledges?"

"Well, no—but he might if—"

"Not without fireworks or him being in a cast from neck to knee." She beamed. "I'll come, the excitement will do me good. It'll be like old times. Now, my dear," she said, taking Kaley's arm and urging her to where the children stood, "allow me to introduce you to Lacy and Jason. Then I'm off. I've lessons to plan and parents to call. The school district's got me running hither and yon teaching homebound, you know."

The children were herded into the front seat of Kaley's truck. Miss Broom waved them off with a reminder for Kaley to remain alert.

Kaley's gaze darted hesitantly toward the children. The boy, Jason, was a cherub, sweet-faced with rosy cheeks and curly blond hair. He stared back at her with an innocent curiosity.

The girl, Lacy, was another matter. She was thin, as if she'd just had a growth spurt that stretched too little skin over bones too long and narrow. Her hair was brown and long and tangled. Her eyes were huge. If she ever grew into them, she'd be a beauty. But one of her eyes was beginning to swell shut.

"Before I take you home," Kaley said, "we'll stop at my place to put some ice and witch hazel on that eye."

"No thanks," the child said tersely.

"Well, we'll have to stop there anyway. I have to put my groceries away first or the ice cream will melt."

"Ice cream?" Jason said, all hope.

Lacy elbowed him. "We don't like ice cream."

"Oh. Gee, that's a shame, because I've invited all of you for supper tonight and that's what we're having for dessert—ice cream with a toasted meringue topping."

"You can't toast ice cream," Lacy said caustically.

"There's a way," Kaley said. "I'm glad you've moved on the mountain. I hope we'll be friends."

"We're not going to be there long. Our mother is coming for us."

"Oh? Where is your mother?"

Lacy glared at Kaley. "None of your business."

Kaley floundered in the face of the child's hostility. "You're right," she said. "It isn't."

"And we probably won't be coming to supper, either. Uncle Slater doesn't like you."

Kaley nearly ran off the road. She jerked the steering column. "How do you know. Did he say that?"

The girl let slip a knowing, secret smile. "Uncle Slater doesn't like anybody," she said with finality.

"But, I do too like ice cream," said Jason.

The turn-off to the farms was blocked by a long-bed truck. Kaley pulled onto the verge. Slater Rutledge was tamping down the dirt around the post of a shiny new mailbox. He tossed aside the posthole digger and moseyed over toward her. On his way he spied the children. He stopped in his tracks and frowned.

"What's going on here?"

"They missed their bus."

The children glanced at their uncle, but did not wait for instructions; they scrambled out of the car, inspected the name he had lettered onto the rural mailbox, then climbed into the bed of the truck, where they stood, looking over the top of the cab as if they were to be trundled off to the guillotine.

Kaley emerged from her car. "I'll see you kids later."

Jason tried to answer. Lacy locked an arm around his neck and pulled him down. Dismayed, Kaley shifted her gaze to Slater.

His hat sat at a rakish angle, shading his face.

"The children don't seem too happy," she said.

"Happy is as happy does," he replied.

Their eyes met and held, while something uncommon, illogical, unbidden went between them.

Kaley imagined him taking her into his arms, pressing her against his chest, whispering in her ear.

Uncle Slater doesn't like you.

She put the fantasy out of her mind. After all, she was nothing if not practical and down-to-earth.

"I suppose you want to know how I came by the kids," she said brightly.

"They'll fill me in."

"I was in town, buying the makings for our supper—"

"Can't make it."

"Can't make it?" Her chin came up, drawing taut the flesh on her neck so that pulse beats in its hollows were visible. Her eyes widened, huge and liquid, shadowy with frustration. She reached out and touched his arm, trying to salvage the unsalvageable. "Please come. I've bought some lovely food—"

"It'll keep." *Neanderthal?* he was thinking. *The two-faced wench.*

"I've invited some friends."

"Yours, not mine."

"Why are you suddenly being so boneheaded?"

"Can't help it, runs in the family." He scowled, offering her an expression that had sent men scurrying and caused women to cross to the other side of the street.

Kaley inhaled. "You've got to come. The children said they want to. I really need to talk to you about my business. I know we can work something out."

Slater pursed his lips. Whatever was going on in that little head of hers was on the wrong side of imprudence. She was stirred up; the rapid rise and fall of her breasts beneath the cotton blouse confirmed it. He cursed silently. He could feel his groin tightening. "I'm always willing to listen."

"If that's true, why refuse my invitation? What are you afraid of?"

"Me? Afraid?" He threw his head back and laughed.

"The trouble between the families was years ago. I don't think it's fair of you to hold that against *me.*"

"The way you tell it, it's old man Jackson with the wild hair up his arse."

"I'm offering you an olive branch."

Observing her, Slater's eyes darkened. The woman thought her looks gave her an edge. He'd met her kind before; they flaunted bosoms and shapely hips, purred to a man's face and lashed out with claws once his back was turned. "My instincts say you're hoping to flay me alive with that olive branch."

"If you think that's true, then don't accept! You want to fling the offer of a kindness back in my face? Fine! As it happens, I have better things to do than waste my time on you!"

"Whoa, missy. Don't get your dander up. I'm only laying out the rules."

"Rules? For what? You're the one who's arrogant, immodest—"

"I don't like modesty. It's almost always fake. I like things out in the open."

"I'm being open with you. What makes you think I'm not?"

"A little bird."

"Move your truck, please," she said, her voice at the cutting edge of anger. "You're blocking the road."

He fished into his pocket, brought up a bit of blue and draped it about her neck. "I believe this belongs to you." His hands rested lightly on her shoulders before he drew his fingertips down the ribbon until they came perilously close to her breasts.

It was not a lingering touch, yet Kaley was conscious of a sudden inexplicable apprehension that seemed like a warning.

"Excuse me," she said, stepping beyond his reach. Her eyes flashed with disdain, camouflage to disguise her reaction to his touch.

"You're welcome," he called softly as she returned to her car.

While he moved his truck, Kaley sat behind the wheel suffering a myriad of emotion. Despair and excitement warred within her. She had forgotten what it was like to want something so badly that longing bordered on obsession.

"What time?" he called to her as she jockeyed her truck past his.

She braked.

"We'll spruce up. What time are you serving?"

She inhaled sharply. "Sundown."

"HOW LONG are we going to have to haul water?" Lacy asked, dragging the bucket over to the wooden counter. "When's the electricity going to be turned on? And when are we going to get a television?"

"Electricity will be on tomorrow." He'd used the time in town to arrange the utilities, buy up building supplies and tucker, and order a fridge. A television had not occurred to him. "Shut up and let me look at that eye."

"Leave me alone. It doesn't hurt."

Slater picked her up and deposited her on the counter. "I'm the boss around here, missy, not you." He inspected her eye, found it sound, but her eye socket was turning shades of blue. "Now, what was the fight about?"

"Nuthin'." She glared at him with her one good eye.

Slater turned to Jason. "All right mate, it's your turn. What was the fight about?"

"The kids said Daddy went to hell, not heaven. They said we was murderers."

"Jason!" Lacy cried.

"Well, they did," he huffed.

Slater rubbed his jaw. "Murderers? And who is it we did this dastardly deed on?"

"Jackson women. They said it's why we had to leave Fentress County."

"We left because the coal ran out and there was no way to make a living grubbing out of rock and shale."

"Aunt Willie said we made a good living perking whiskey," Lacy disputed.

"We didn't kill anyone. A visitor to the homeplace got tipsy, missed the switchback going downhill and plowed into some neighbor women who were hanging out clothes. He killed them."

"Was it our fault?" Lacy asked, curious.

"No. The man hit a tree and killed himself, too. But old man Jackson was so mad he went and shot the fellow to pieces anyway. They say there was little more than shredded shirt and buttons left to bury."

Jason looked scared. "Will he shoot us, too?"

"Hell, no. That was a long time ago."

"People still talk about it," Lacy said.

"Learning you're a Rutledge just got the gossip going again. It'll stop."

Lacy sniffed. "Suppose it don't?"

"Then I reckon I'll have to patch up your other eye, missy."

"We don't want to live here," she cried. "There're no kids to play with, no houses to trick or treat—"

"You've tucker and a roof over your heads," Slater told them, exasperated.

Lacy looked up. Slater had patched the hole with tin. "Not much of a roof, or walls, either."

Slater pointed to the hammer, nails and saws piled into a corner. "Help yourself to the job, missy."

Jason said, "Do you think Daddy is in hell?"

Uncharitably Slater thought: *I hope so.* "No, all Rutledges go to heaven. It's a tradition."

"Are we going to eat at Kaley Jackson's?" Lacy asked with deliberate indifference.

"I am," Slater said. "You won't, unless you cut the sass."

"I don't like her."

"If you don't learn to use a little guile," Slater told her, "you're going to grow up to be an old maid like Aunt Willie."

"I like Kaley," announced Jason. "She knows little guys *love* ice cream."

With her one good eye, Lacy deposited a pitying look on her brother. "It's a bribe, stupid."

Chapter Four

Kaley glanced beyond Independent to the family plot. The white and gray headstones were turning purple in the shadows. She wished a ghost of some long-dead Jackson would materialize and offer her a solution. Although, with the way fate was misusing her, it'd probably be the spirit of Stubborn Jackson, whose propensity for digging his heels in was legendary. Her gaze shifted back to Independent.

"Please, at least trim your beard and put on a clean shirt."

"What for? A man don't have to spruce up to shoot somebody. Where'd you hide my buckshot?"

"Where you'll never find it."

He grunted. "Suit yourself. There's more 'n one way to skin a polecat."

Kaley sighed wearily. "You're holding on to this grievance all out of proportion. It wasn't a Rutledge who drove the car that killed—"

"It was their rotgut whiskey that done it. They fed it—"

"You make whiskey!"

"Sure I do, but I temper it with time. I ain't never drunk it or sold it raw! And that's what those fool Rutledges did! They killed my women and stoppered my business. The sheriff raked over these hills with so many hounds wasn't a cave or holler left could hide a still."

"Why don't you admit *that's* what sticks in your craw. You had to go to farming corn and pumpkins instead of making moonshine. You've been ranting and raving for thirty years—"

" 'Tain't no longer than a bank holds a mortgage."

Kaley threw up her hands in disgust. "Slater Rutledge had nothing to do with Sarah and Lou Ann's accident, so save your wit for the dinner table. Miss Broom will swoon all over you."

"Thelma Broom ain't the swoonin' type. An' I told ye, I ain't sitting to table with no Rutledge."

"This is my house, too, Independent. I have the right to have whomever I want as guests."

"It's a right you took. I ain't offered it."

"Well, fine. When Jessie goes back to town tonight, I'll go with her. And tomorrow I'll march right over to the Inn and tell all your old cronies you put me out."

"That'd be a lie!" he huffed, pride dangling. "I ain't never set no womenfolk out on the street to fend for herself. If ye insist on having the enemy to sup, do it! But you'll rue the day you laid eyes on a Rutledge. They ain't nuthin' but trouble."

"And you're not?" she asked angrily. "You worry your memories like an old bone. You hold them up to the present all out of context. Bury them and call it a day!"

"I did bury 'em, name of Sary and Lou Ann!"

Fury blazing from his faded eyes, he turned and ambled off, dragging his left foot in his hip-shot gait, his useless shotgun cradled in his arms.

The knot in Kaley's stomach was reminiscent of all the times she had failed to live up to her parents' expectations. All day long she'd thought sundown was never coming, and now that it was upon her, nothing was going right.

Perhaps when she arrived, Miss Broom could coax the old man into the house. If only he would meet Slater, then maybe...

Oh, hang it! The old goat was so settled in his thoughts and ways, it'd take a miracle, or death, to put him off.

She went back into the house.

It was in pristine order. She'd made up table decorations out of dried wild flowers; vegetables warmed in the oven, and the roast was on the sideboard ready to be carved. The moment she heard a car door slam, she'd set fire to the tinder in the fireplace.

She'd debated the use of candles, finally discarding the idea as ostentatious—and with Jessie and Miss Broom coming—obvious. No right-minded mountain woman lighted a candle unless the electricity went off or she had no electricity to begin with.

A log fire and homemade scuppernong wine would have to do for ambiance.

She went into her bedroom and took one last look at her reflection.

She'd dressed simply—navy slacks, white blouse and navy cardigan. Her only splash of color was the red ribbon that tamed her hair, tied at the nape. This was, after all—as much a business meal as welcome celebration.

She looked exceptionally pale. Kaley stared at herself for a long moment, then she unbuttoned the top two buttons on her blouse.

Somewhere deep within, she was shocked at her own audacity.

Still, the only way she'd be able to match Slater's naked insolence was to answer the door wearing nothing but her apron. The thought put such a glow in her cheeks that when Jessie and Miss Broom arrived, Miss Broom exclaimed how flushed her face was.

"Hurrying does it," the elderly teacher insisted. "You young people try to do everything at the last minute. Makes me think of lemmings. A body wonders if you're all not rushing through life just to try on eternity for size."

"Where's this paragon of a man who's got you feeling untethered?" Jessie asked as she slipped out of her jacket. "I'm ready to be impressed."

"He hasn't arrived yet, and I'm not untethered," Kaley told her, voice silken.

Jessie grinned and went over to the sideboard, inspecting the array of food. "My, my," she cooed, casting Kaley a sly smile. "Aren't we the vixen?"

"I know what you're thinking," Kaley said feebly, "and it's utterly insane. I'm not trying to woo the man—except to allow me to harvest grapevines."

Jessie plucked a fat olive from the tray and popped it into her mouth. "I believe you. It's a best friend's duty to believe—"

"Where's Independent?" Miss Broom asked after she, too, passed approval of the laden sideboard.

"In his shack," Kaley told her. "I was hoping you could coax him in. If he would just meet Slater Rutledge..."

Miss Broom snorted. "I won't even try. One thing, among many, you young people don't understand about us older folks is that we *enjoy* our malice. It keeps our minds keen, makes us feel useful. What with the Rutledge boy back on the mountain, Independent must be in top form." Miss Broom smiled sweetly. "But I will go say hello."

Via the kitchen window, Kaley watched the elderly teacher clump across the backyard toward the shack. Beyond Miss Broom and the drying sheds, Kaley's eye caught a movement. Shadowy at first, but then they burst out of the forest, the children running ahead.

Shade and shadow dappled him, but there was no mistaking the size and magnificence of Slater Rutledge.

Her heart leaped, and an involuntary gasp escaped her, which brought Jessie from the dining area to look over her shoulder.

The trio of Rutledges had momentarily stopped at the Jackson family plot.

"Oh, my," Jessie murmured. "That's a man I'd diet for. I don't see his wife with him."

"There isn't a wife," Kaley said, unable to keep hidden the ineffable satisfaction that fact gave her.

"Really?" Jessie said. "How'd you discover that?"

"Miss Broom told me. The children are his niece and nephew. Their father is dead, their mother is apparently out of the picture."

"And you're ready to leap into the breach. Don't deny it. I can see your antennas swirling."

"I think it's lovely to have children around."

"Well, just be careful you don't sentence yourself to a life of grief."

"Now, what is that supposed to mean?"

Jessie patted her on the shoulder. "Nothing, a twinge of envy surfaced is all. Euphoria looks terrific on you. Go on out and greet your guests, they look as if they mean to stay out in the cemetery until they've an accurate body count."

Kaley went toward Slater. He was standing at the foot of Virgil's grave, his face looking as if it had been chiseled whole from hardwood.

"My husband," she said, approaching him, and then found herself under his scrutiny. He was studying her as if deciding her fate and destiny in one fell swoop.

After a heartbeat, he said. "How old was he? Thirty-six?"

"Almost."

He shook his head. "My brother was forty-two. Dying is hard on everybody, robs you of your illusions."

Kaley was nonplussed. "Somehow I hadn't placed sensitive sentiment in your realm."

"Why not?" Between the gloom and the deep shadow of his hat brim, his expression wasn't clear, but the lifted eyebrow was in his tone.

She paused. "Because of the way we met?"

He laughed. "You don't sound too sure, missy." He paused, glancing once more about the small graveyard. "Your parents?"

She averted her face and frowned. "Alive and well and living in Florida."

"Did I barrel in where angels fear to tread?"

"Not really. My mother and I aren't on the best of terms just now." She gave up a small smile. "C'mon. Jessie and Miss Broom are waiting to meet you."

"And the old man?"

She shook her head. "I'm sorry. Independent is being a stick-in-the-mud."

He whistled to the children, who were gamboling over and around headstones, then casually, with a hand at the small of her back, he urged Kaley along. "Whatever you're cooking smells good. It had my nose twitching a quarter mile away."

His hand burned its imprint into her spine. Kaley felt on fire. A wonderful, terrible sensation.

"How long were you married?" he asked.

"Five years."

"Children?"

"No."

"You don't like children?"

"Of course I do!"

"Good, I have two I'll let go cheap."

"I'll make an offer after I've seen their table manners."

He faked a groan. "That'd be too late, missy. By then I'd have to pay you."

She held open the door for Jason and Lacy to file through. Jason smiled up at her shyly, but Lacy's gaze pierced her. It brought a halt to the sliver of feminine warmth she was basking in.

She tried to tell herself that she had not seen spite and malice in the child's features. That perhaps the swollen and bruised eye gave menace where none was meant. She made an effort to greet the girl pleasantly. "I'm glad you came, Lacy."

Lacy's answer was to roll her eyes ceilingward.

Kaley sighed and settled on allowing a friendship to develop naturally—if it would.

"Jessie," she called, "come and meet my new neighbors."

"THE OUTBACK IS HARSH," Slater replied to a question Jessie had put to him. "There are areas that are like an oasis, but not the mining towns or the stations. It's mud or dust and little in between."

"I read a book once about floods in Australia," Miss Broom put in.

"I lived through a couple of 'wets' that gave me an appreciation for Mother Nature," Slater said with a grin. "Got caught in a flash flood during a mustang roundup and had to fight the snakes and 'roos for a spot of high ground."

Jessie and Miss Broom were captivated. Kaley was fighting the sensation of falling under his spell and failing miserably. The sound of his voice was compelling, drawing her in. His large hands were expressive while he talked of gold and diamonds and opals. She couldn't seem to keep her eyes off his hands.

"A two-thousand-carat black opal found during Halley's Comet's 1985 visit was named after the comet. When it was finally estimated, it topped out at three million dollars."

Miss Broom eyed him speculatively. "Came home a comer, didn't you, boy?"

He laughed. "I tried. But not to the tune of three million."

He glanced at Kaley. Her face was flushed, her eyes aglow, tendrils of hair shadowed her neck, calling attention to the veins throbbing in its hollows. She looked provocative as hell. His flesh felt suddenly restless, and he had to ask Miss Broom to repeat herself.

"Your aunt, Wilhelmina? Is that old spinster still alive? I haven't heard from her in years."

He leaned back in his chair. "Aunt Willie is laid up with a broken leg at the moment, but she'll be along before year's end. I'll tell her you asked about her."

"It'll be nice to have another woman on the mountain," Kaley said, wishing for some way to relieve the tension she was suffering. She smiled at the children. No help there. They were exceptionally quiet. She suspected their behavior was on direct orders from Slater.

Finally Miss Broom put down her fork, and Kaley brought out the baked Alaska to appreciative ooohs and aaahs.

"You cook good," Lacy said grudgingly.

"I wish you lived at our house," Jason said. "Then I could ask for seconds."

Kaley scooped him up another serving before he was chastised. She looked at Slater. "Another helping?"

"Thanks, no."

"I'll make some fresh coffee."

"None for me," Miss Broom said, and began making excuses to leave. Kaley panicked.

"Not yet, it's early."

Miss Broom was not to be deterred.

"Tomorrow's a workday," Jessie said.

"Jessie," Kaley pleaded as her friend hurried to catch up with Miss Broom.

"What can I say? I rode with Miss Broom. You outdid yourself tonight, Kaley. Everything was terrific."

Behind her, Slater was ordering Lacy and Jason to don their jackets.

Kaley turned. "I was hoping..." she began, trailing off.

She'd not had one private word with him!

Damn! Damn! Damn! She had gone and done the stupid thing of inviting the world to dine. All because she was a little bit frightened—of herself, of her own inner turmoil. She was no closer to harvesting grapevines tonight than she had been yesterday!

Attempting to salvage the evening, she threw a shawl about her shoulders and accompanied Slater and the children as far as the cemetery.

Lacy, freed from constraint, prodded Jason ahead, playing hide-and-seek among the tombstones.

"It's turned cool," Slater said, making conversation. "Winter's in the offing. I can sense it."

Kaley found her opening. "I hope this warm spell holds. I can get in more harvesting."

"I'm thinking of running some stables, raising a few horses," he said.

"That's great. My work wouldn't interfere—"

"It would," he disputed.

"It won't!"

"It would, missy. You'd be a distraction."

"For a horse?" she said icily.

He stopped. "For a horse, a flea, a man." His hands were suddenly at her bosom, fingering the buttons on her blouse. "What was this supposed to do? Entrap me?"

"No." In a headlong fluster, Kaley stepped back, stumbling over the roots of a tree.

"Careful there," he cooed, his hands moving quickly, forcefully to balance her, somehow managing along the way to position her back against the tree.

"I'm fine now. Thank you." Trying to appear unaffected, she brushed at her elbows.

"I'm not fine, Kaley. You've tantalized and teased me all evening, looking at me with soulful bedroom eyes, brushing up against me when you were serving, touching my leg with yours under the table..."

"I didn't! Not on purpose."

"No?"

"No!"

"I hate to show you up a liar, missy, but..." An arm tightened about her, his mouth hovered near hers, his breath warm on her face.

"Stop this," she uttered hoarsely.

"You don't want me to stop."

She felt his breath shape every word. "Yes...I do."

"Slap my face, missy."

"What?"

"Kick my shins."

"You're crazy!" she accused, feeling as if she were being held together by a weak rubber band. She closed her eyes for a split second, not so much to succumb, but to gather her wits.

He traced the shape of her mouth with a fingertip. "Tell me to keep my hands to myself, missy."

The invisible band broke. Her flesh tingled. "Keep... keep your hands to yourself," she repeated, voice barely audible.

His thumb moved from her lips to her ear to her eyelids.

"That feel good, missy?"

There was a panic inside her body, an excruciating awareness of him, his nearness. "What do you want me to say?" she whispered.

"Yes or no." Slater looked at the slow rise and fall of her breasts and had the idea that she would be astonishing in bed—lovely and surprising and ardent.

She faltered. "Yes."

His belt buckle was pressing against her, and so was... Her throat went dry. He was fully aroused and making certain she was aware of his arousal. She was aware too, of the width of his chest, the power in his arm that locked her to him.

"And this?" he said, planting a butterfly kiss on first one eyelid then the other."

"Just...just ordinary," she told him, trying for levity to put them back on more neutral territory.

"Just ordinary, missy?" he said, voice gritty. "Well, hell, I never did like being just ordinary."

He lowered his mouth to hers.

It was unlike any kiss Kaley had ever experienced. His tongue prowled and probed with such savage mastery that she was devoid of gravity, soaring, her senses spinning. The kiss was a language beyond the limits of verbal expression. It spoke of longing and desire that matched her own. Her eyes closed as if she were trying to absorb the aftermath of shock her thoughts caused, and even as she responded, something wild and wonderful rose and blossomed within her. Had she not been pinned within his muscular arms she knew she would've collapsed.

A lifetime later he released her mouth, though his hands continued to wreak all manner of havoc on her nervous system as they moved over her back to clasp her waist.

"You know what this is, missy?" he asked softly, his hard glance deep and penetrating.

Unable to utter a sound, Kaley shook her head.

"It's called finding yourself between a rock and a hard place." He meant the comment more for himself than Kaley. "Just being this near you is a drain on my common sense." He wondered how he could get so worked up over a woman when his every thought and act was supposed to be upon home and hearth and self-preservation. *Think about what you're doing,* he warned himself. Abruptly he dropped his hand, freeing her. "I'll concede you this, Kaley Jackson, you're one beautiful piece of goods."

To Kaley, he sounded disappointed, as if she were guilty of some infraction of the rules, *his* rules. Utterly confused, she slumped against the tree. The bark was cold and rough, jolting her into a measure of reality.

"Why did you do that?" she cried breathlessly.

"Wanted to."

"But what were you hoping to accomplish?"

"Not a thing. Take it as my thanks for supper."

"Is that how they do it in Australia?" Her voice broke.

He laughed, and Kaley heard the sound as the smug satisfaction of conquest.

Clarity tumbled through her brain. "You never had any intention of allowing me to harvest grapevines on your property, did you?"

"Would you let me pasture horses on Jackson land?"

"That would be for Independent to say. The land's not mine."

"We both know what the old man's answer would be, don't we?"

"But that has nothing to do with me!"

"Well, missy, somehow, it doesn't seem quite right—calling us Rutledges murderers on the one hand, and asking us for charity with the other." Somewhere nearby a cricket sounded, a harsh salute to his words.

Kaley was dumbfounded. "Charity! I'm willing to pay you a portion of my profits!"

"Don't need your money, missy."

Kaley rubbed her hand over her eyes. "If you knew what your answer would be, why didn't you tell me? Why let me hope?"

"Have been telling you—politely. You haven't been listening."

Her hackles rose. She had been listening, but with heart and soul, not her mind. "I just don't see how it would hurt for me to harvest vines—"

"Well, missy, the way I learned it, a man has to depend on his own resources. Rutledge land is my resource, my territory. I'm going to be using it. So, you can't."

"Coming to supper, pouring on the charm for Miss Broom and Jessie and me—was that just more charade?" she quizzed angrily.

"I was just being neighborly. Next time, it'll be my turn to put up the tucker." He reached out and drew a fingertip lightly from her earlobe to the pounding vein in her neck. "Night, missy. Pleasant dreams."

"You deserve your reputation!" she yelped hoarsely, throwing the words at his back.

He whistled, the children popped out from behind a nearby tree, and Kaley suspected they'd witnessed the entire scene between herself and Slater.

Mortified on more than one account, she spun around and hurried toward the house.

An elongated shadow crossed her path. In the next instant the shadow had substance and was talking.

"Now, ain't that a fine thing! Throwed yourself at a Rutledge atop of Virgil's grave!"

Kaley glared at her grandfather-in-law. "Get away from me. I'm sick of men! Old men, young men, dead men, and anything in between!"

"Refused you, ain't he?"

Kaley pulled ahead.

"See, even a Rutledge don't want a citified woman with highfalutin ideas."

The porch light cast a yellow glow. Kaley stood in it, the control she held over herself in dire certainty of shredding. "You want me to fix you a plate of food?"

"Naw. I'd druther eat Flossie's rations than the leavin's at a table set for a Rutledge."

She went into the house and slammed the door after her. Hard.

Slater Rutledge had made a fool out of her on purpose!

Heard you coming from a mile off, missy.

He had set the stage, and certain of his audience, played her with the disarming skill of a virtuoso. Dunce that she was, she had made it easy for him.

He knew very well Independent had been watching, and the children, too.

He was hateful, inconsiderate, selfish, and morally warped.

The taste of him lingered on her lips.

The craving to be loved and wanted, to be held dear came on strong. In that context she no longer thought of Virgil as the center of her existence.

She looked down at her lap, reliving the sensation of Slater's arousal pressed against her.

Oh, give it up, she told herself. *Things are the way they are. It is just a game to him.*

Game or not, feminine insight intruded.

He couldn't turn his senses off any more than she could.

She hoped he was in agony.

The thought gave her a small sense of satisfaction.

THE DOME OF TREES hugging the path between the homesteads seemed to create a hush. It fit Slater's mood. He gave the flashlight to Lacy and allowed the children to run ahead and explore.

Bit by bit Kaley's image crossed his mind's eye. Her dark hair tied back from her face, with tendrils curling about her ears, and the promise of passion reined in that vibrated from her, would make any man take notice. Damn, but he couldn't seem to keep his hands off her.

That was bad news.

Getting caught up with Kaley Jackson was outside all boundaries of good sense.

To add to this agitation, earlier in the day he'd discovered the old man lurking about the borders of Rutledge property. Aunt Willie had cautioned him that should he find Independent Jackson still alive, not to forget the man was an old rooster with his comb bent out of shape.

It didn't seem right—if the old geezer was holding on to a grievance about his womenfolk, and discovered a Rutledge kissing Kaley—why wasn't he taking up the cudgels for her? It smacked of peculiar loyalties.

Kaley.

Buried deep in the recesses of his mind was the expectation that one day he'd marry, build a house, raise kids—*grow old*...

He muttered a curse.

Jason ran back to him. "Did you see a snake?"

"No, a ghost."

Jason shivered. "A real ghost? One from the cemetery?"

"No, a ghost of past dreams."

The boy lost interest and raced back to his sister.

A few more strides and Slater's thoughts were once again on Kaley and himself. He couldn't stop thinking about that moment when he had put his mouth to hers. He'd been suspended, finding himself on the brink of believing that all things were possible.

Even miracles.

He frowned.

Kaley Jackson couldn't stop what was growing inside his skull.

He was going to have to get past this.

Chapter Five

The door to the drying shed burst open. The blast of air was frigid. Kaley spun around. Her mouth lifted in an uncertain smile.

Slater Rutledge filled the doorway, standing there as still as a store-window mannequin. He had changed his mind! He'd thought about her all night and now he was here to tell her he adored her, that he was hopelessly in love with her, that she was a dream come true, that she could harvest his land...

"Grab your shovel, missy."

"What?" He didn't sound besotted. In fact, his tone was one of controlled fury. She took a closer look at his face. His mouth was tight, his eyes blazing with a dangerous ferocity. She backed up to the worktable where she'd been packing grapevines. "Close that door."

"Close it? Were I as vindictive as you, I'd yank the bloody thing off its hinges."

"Vindictive? I haven't done anything." The thought dashed through her mind that the prudent thing to do was to move to the other side of the worktable. It wasn't much of a barrier—not as effective as a moat, but better than nothing.

His eyes tracked her as she moved. "You're a poor liar, missy. We proved that last night."

"All *we* proved last night is that you're a bully," she said silkily, discomfited at being reminded how he'd plundered her mouth, since it was now obvious he wasn't anywhere near to declaring love. "You can't just come barreling in here, making accusations. And put that cigar out. The smell will get into my plants." She lifted her hand, drawing his eye to the rafters from which all manner of flowers, grasses, and weeds hung in rows of wild array.

The cigar stayed lighted. Slater puffed on it. "I never could countenance a woman who was intolerant of a few manly pleasures. And I'm not making accusations, I'm talking fact."

He closed the distance between them in several long strides, knocking aside the heavy cardboard boxes filled with dried and coiled vines. "Get your shovel."

"I can't think of anything about which I owe you an explanation," she said while sidling crabwise to the far end of her worktable. "Why don't you calm down and tell me what has you in an uproar."

"Because that wouldn't feel so satisfying as this—" He feinted as if aiming for one direction, then moved fluidly in the other to corner her between the table and the wall.

"Now then," he said, picking her up and tossing her over his shoulder.

"Wha— Hey!" Kaley squealed. "You idiot! Put me down." She began to pound and flail his back with her fists.

"A little to the left below my shoulder blade," he said of her pounding. "Got a sore spot there."

"Goat! Libertine!" she wailed, bombarding him with every vile name that came to mind while he just stood there waiting patiently for the tirade to come to a halt. Finally, reluctantly, Kaley stopped struggling and allowed her body to sag.

"That's better." He looked around, spied a shovel among the tools in a pile of burlap in a corner, grabbed it and strode out the door. He kicked it closed with a boot heel.

"Door's closed," he said.

"I always did like a man with dry wit," she said, coating every syllable with a thick layer of sarcasm. "You've made your point. You're faster than I am, stronger than I am, and bigger than I am. You're one of the anointed few—now *put me down.*"

"Shut up."

"You're making a fool out of yourself."

"Better the fool than a self-righteous hypocrite."

"If Independent sees what you're doing, he'll shoot you."

His scathing laughter was muffled. "Hope he doesn't try for a head shot, missy, 'cause if he misses, he'll hit you in your sweet little rear."

She made a grab for the shovel handle.

"Tut, tut, none of that," he said, as if he had eyes in the back of his head.

Kaley caught the shift in his tone. "You're enjoying doing this to me," she assailed.

"Right as rain, missy. The pleasure is all mine."

Grabbing a handful of his jacket and using it as leverage, she raised up, trying to see where he was taking her. Onto the switchback.

"If you're planning to tear off my clothes and force yourself on me in the woods, you have another think coming!"

He laughed. The sound was deep and rich and reverberated off the surrounding hills. "Bite your tongue, missy."

He aimed himself *down* the mountain toward the highway.

"I'm capable of walking," she pleaded.

"You're getting a free ride. Settle down."

"I'm going to be sick!"

"Think again," he warned.

"I'm cold!"

He stopped, held the shovel between his knees, put a hand beneath her jacket, pulled her shirttail out and ran his hand up her spine.

Kaley yelped. His hand was cold and callused.

"You feel warm as toast to me, missy."

He retrieved the shovel and continued his way down the lane. Kaley grabbed at an overhanging tree branch.

"For shame," Slater said, and did a side step, keeping it just out of her reach. "You're a regular virago, missy, and here I was, thinking 'Slater, old boy, you've really hit the mother lode with Kaley Jackson.' Yessir...saw you sliding down that shale and thought, what a sweet, fulsome wood sprite. But now

I know you were packaged by the wicked witch just to annoy me.''

''Save the fairy tales for Jason and Lacy.''

''Good idea. Comfortable?''

''Not very, but thank you for asking. I'm going to kill you first chance I get, Slater. I want you to know that.''

He laughed again. ''Sure, honey—'' He bit down on his cigar. He'd almost blurted that she'd have to beat the doctors to do it.

She raised her head, looked at the back of his neck. It was tanned and corded. His hair was wound in a thong and hung down his back. It smelled of soap. She yanked it. ''Put me down!''

Slater winced. ''Stop that or you'll earn a spanking.''

''With your sick mind, that would probably turn you on, wouldn't it?''

''Might, might not. Keep yanking on my hair and you'll soon find out.''

With a ragged sigh of resignation Kaley sagged and gave herself up to the ignoble act of being carted downhill like a sack of potatoes.

He dumped her in the dust on the highway verge, next to his uprooted mailbox. While she sat there gathering her wits, he tossed the shovel at her feet.

''Replant it,'' he ordered, pointing to his mailbox.

Kaley picked up both herself and the shovel. ''I can use this as a weapon.''

His smile was solid and saintlike, his words steely. ''Give it your best shot on the first try, missy.''

"I didn't knock your mailbox down. A car probably did it."

"Awfully selective car. Yours is still standing and they aren't more than a dozen inches apart."

Dragging the shovel, Kaley went over to the downed box and glanced at the surrounding verge. There were no tire tacks.... A yard or so away in the weeds she spied it—a pile of fresh manure—Flossie! And where Flossie went, Independent went. Her shoulders sagged.

Reining in her rage, she turned to Slater.

"All right. I accept the blame."

"Good girl." He leaned against a jutting rock face, peeled a fresh cigar, lighted it, then folded his arms like a warden over a chain gang. "Now, dig."

Once she'd dug the hole large enough to fit the mailbox post, she glanced at him. His eyes were locked upon her, as if in a trance. She saw in his face the same desperate ache of longing she felt deep inside her own soul. For an instant his eyes continued to caress her, then he threw down his cigar and ground it out beneath his boot. "I'll trust you to finish it," he said, and left her to it.

"FOOLING WITH A MAILBOX is a federal offense!"

Independent gave her a careless grin. "'Twas an accident. Flossie kicked it over."

"Why didn't you fix it?"

"Forgot. Memory's not what it use to be."

Kaley displayed the palms of her hands. "See these blisters? They're my reward for your hatefulness."

He grunted. "Any ninny knows ye orta wear gloves working a spade."

"If you keep vandalizing his property, he's going to catch you."

"I can take care of myself."

A sudden gust of wind rattled the treetops. Kaley shivered.

"Be snowing afore the end of the week," Independent predicted. "If ye ain't got anything more to chaw about," he said, tugging on Flossie's halter, "I got to get my pumpkins harvested."

Kaley clenched her fists, regretting it at once. "Stay away from Slater Rutledge," she warned.

"Har! Ain't me who's cozyin' up to him."

Kaley opened her mouth to protest, then closed it. There was no use trying to convince Independent that she had no interest whatsoever in Slater Rutledge—mostly because she was having difficulty convincing herself.

"I DON'T UNDERSTAND why you aren't taking umbrage," Jessie said.

Kaley got up to add another log to the fire. Outside, the first damp flakes of snow swirled in the air. "I did take umbrage—but with Independent. He's the one who did the deed. Slater was only reacting."

"Some reaction. Throwing you over his shoulder like a caveman."

"Oh, that wasn't the worst part. The worst came after I'd no more than got this mailbox up than the mail carrier drove up and handed me a letter from my folks. Talk about puncturing my balloon..."

"Was it edged in black?"

Kaley sighed. "Might as well have been. They footnoted it—that if I continued to live up here doing nothing with my life, they have no intention of throwing good money after bad on me—I'm to be disinherited."

"Would they?"

"Probably. But it's not the money, it's the validation. I'm doing what I love doing. I don't want to live in Florida. The only way to know the seasons change is the mail carriers go from short pants to long. I don't want to live with them. I don't want to be mother's good girl for the rest of my life. Anyway, I couldn't just go off and leave Independent."

"Or your barbaric caveman?" Jessie said coyly.

Recalling the way he'd looked at her, Kaley was unexpectedly choked by emotion. "He's not barbaric, not really." Day and night his face floated above her thoughts and imprinted itself on her brain.

"So that's how it is," Jessie acknowledged. "Have you seen him since the episode with the mailbox?"

"Only in the distance. He's had building supplies delivered, electricity installed. I've seen the trucks going up and down the switchback."

"What about the kids?"

"I see them going to and from the bus stop. I try to talk with them. Jason is a cherub...so sweet, but Lacy is a stone wall. She sashays on past with her nose in the air."

"Work on her, she'll come around. Has Slater come to borrow a cup of sugar yet?"

Kaley gave an abbreviated laugh. "Don't be silly."

"Have you taken over a casserole?"

"I had them to dinner!"

"Well, that was business—wasn't it?"

"I suppose."

"Seems to me," Jessie said, "you're at a point where you're going to have to take charge of this affair."

Kaley's head jerked. "We're not having an affair."

Jessie smiled. "Sweetie, you are, but at the moment, it's all in your head. Don't deny it. I've been there. Either assert yourself, or call it a day. Speaking of which, I've got to get over to the Broudy's and try to talk the missus into having her baby in the hospital."

"Mrs. Broudy's having trouble?"

"No, but she needs the rest. This is her fifth." Jessie reached into her bag. "Here's some calcium for Independent. See if you can get him to take it."

"That'll be the day."

"Find his jug and drop a few in. He won't know the difference."

Kaley threw a jacket over her shoulders to walk Jessie to her car. Once outside, she held her face up to the sky. "I love this time of year."

"That's because you can stay inside and be toasty warm. For me it's colds, pneumonia, measles and mumps." Jessie's expression sobered. "I'm sorry about your folks. Maybe if you spend Christmas with them . . ."

"I couldn't bear it—imitation tree, air-conditioning, and mother always *orders* her dinner catered from a fancy restaurant. That's so the smell of turkey doesn't permeate thc house. Christmas up here . . . it's the real thing. This is Mark Twain and Sergeant York country. We have atmosphere. Did you know Mark Twain was conceived in Jamestown?''

Jessie rolled her eyes. ''A history lesson I can do without. But speaking of conceiving brings to mind those two orphans Slater has,'' Jessie said slyly. ''I wonder if he even thinks about holidays like Halloween and Thanksgiving and Christmas.''

The thud of a hammer rang out in the distance. Kaley turned toward the sound. Jessie assessed her friend, seeing the longing in her face as if it were bold print.

''He never stops,'' Kaley said. ''He saws and hammers from dawn to after dark.''

''A man as busy as that probably needs reminding of the holidays, perhaps even some help with the kids' presents. Poor little tykes, I might even call on them myself.''

Kaley gave her friend a wan smile. ''You're suggesting I go over there and let him feed me crow.''

Jessie smiled. ''Better you than him. Sounds like he wears his pride like a suit of armor.''

Kaley smiled. ''And I don't?''

Jessie laughed. ''Nah. Yours is more gauzy and soft.''

After the nurse left, Kaley crunched through the snow up the switchback toward Slater's. Halfway there, she turned around and retraced her steps home. She felt too emotionally raw to face him. And anyway, she didn't like going empty-handed.

Everything—her parents' attitude, Independent's behavior, the dips and struggles in her business, even the loneliness—had all been bearable until Slater Rutledge arrived. Her business had been her anchor. What she felt for Slater had turned her world upside down. Now, she was at sea—lost.

She didn't like the feeling.

Slater's hammer rang out again... and again. The steady rhythm brought images into her mind of thrusting hips and passionate embraces.

I'm sick, she thought.

An hour later, curled in front of the fire, her gaze shifted from the dancing flames to the *Fentress Courier* scattered about her feet.

The photo of a farmer with his prize pumpkin on the front page stared back at her.

An idea struck.

She vacillated for a few seconds, considering it.

It was friendly. Brash. Stupid.

What difference did that make? She had a corner on stupidity.

She went to find Independent. She found him in a barn crib spreading hay. He raised the pitchfork, halfway pointing it at her.

"Don't come near me. I seen Jessie's car. Toss in that pile of floor scrapings whatever she give you to shove down my throat."

"I'm not here on Jessie's behalf—or your health. I need some pumpkins, at least two, no—four. Two to make pumpkin bread and nut cookies, so it doesn't matter their shape, but the other two..." She spied a row of pumpkins almost buried beneath some loose hay. "Like those. They're perfectly shaped and sit level." She moved toward them.

"Get outta there!"

"I just want to—"

"I'm makin' use of them myself."

Kaley bent down and looked closer. The tops had been cut out and replaced so skillfully that the cut seam was barely visible. She picked up the cap of one by its stem and reared back. "Whew!"

"Dang it Kaley Jackson! I told ye—leave it be. You probably done ruined it."

"What is it?"

"It's gonna be pumpkin brandy—if you'd keep your nose out of it."

Kaley eyed him. "To sell?"

"Naw—Christmas gifts," he said, trailing out the sarcasm as far as he could take it.

"I see. Okay, I need two just like those, and two that are good and ripe."

He eyed her warily. "You ain't goin' to tear into me tarnation to hell for making whiskey?"

"Is it good?"

He preened. "The best."

"You have an extra pint lying about anywhere?"

"Might," he said carefully. "Might not."

"I want a pint." She watched his surprise give way to mulling it over.

"Cost ye a dollar."

"Ten cents. You've been slipping into my kitchen and dipping into my sugar to make it."

"I'll put it in the basin on the back porch."

"The dime will be there. Don't forget the pumpkins."

He hooked a thumb in his overalls. "Them will cost ye."

"I already paid. The last time you used the truck to go into town, you didn't fill up the gas tank."

He scowled. "City women make me gag."

The following morning Kaley was up before dawn. She worked in the drying sheds until daybreak, then spent the remainder of the morning and afternoon in her kitchen.

Now and again she went onto the back porch. The mountain was strangely silent today. She missed the sound of Slater's hammer ringing out. Perhaps the snow had driven him indoors, she thought.

At dusk everything was ready and packed on the front seat of her truck. Before she pulled out she went around to Independent's shack and peeked into a dusty, snow-trimmed window. He was snoozing in a lumpy old chair, his stockinged feet propped on an upturned box near his potbellied stove. Thankfully he was in for the night, which meant he wouldn't be spying or making a nuisance of himself.

As she carefully maneuvered the truck toward Slater's, she smiled. Sleeping, the old windbag looked like an aging elf, sweet-faced and bearded. She could never leave him on his own.

As she neared the Rutledge homestead her smile gave way to apprehension. The most Slater could do was ask her to leave.

She would, but by damn not before she waved nut cookies and pumpkin bread under his nose! She hadn't spent all day slaving in the kitchen just to have him toss her on her ear like some uninvited tramp.

Kaley held the thought so close that when the door was opened to her, she was almost, but not quite, hostile.

With Lacy, there was no "almost" about it. She seethed with it. "You can't come in," she said firmly upon opening the door.

"Trick or treat," Kaley said.

For a brief instant Lacy's eyes widened. "We don't have anything to give out."

"I didn't think you would, so I brought you a treat."

Lacy shook her head. "We can't take it."

"I'm not a stranger to you, Lacy. Call your uncle."

"He's sick in bed and we're not to disturb him." She began pushing the door closed.

Sick? Kaley was at once bursting with curiosity and concern, but a glance at Lacy's stern, mouselike visage told her not to voice it. Her arms ladened, Kaley leaned into the doorwell, preventing Lacy from closing her out.

Jason materialized from behind the door to stand behind his sister. "Did you really bring us a Halloween treat?"

"Pumpkin bread and nut cookies, and a pumpkin for each of you to carve out," Kaley told him. "And the makings for hot chocolate—with marshmallows."

"Let her in, Lacy, please," Jason pleaded in a whisper to his sister. "We'll be quiet. We haven't had hot chocolate in years and years."

"We have so," she said angrily, but Kaley saw the girl vacillating.

She shoved the cardboard box into Lacy's arms. Whispering, she said, "You hold on to this, I'll get the other from the truck," and did so with alacrity lest Lacy lock her out. She put the pumpkins on the floor near the hearth where the fire had died to embers.

Her nose picked up the complicated odors of kerosene, stove polish and sawdust, and everywhere there was evidence of Slater's handiwork. Unpainted new wood gleamed on walls, tongue-and-groove slats filled in floors, and above the smoke-darkened ceiling beams a new tin roof glistened in the glow of new electric wall sconces.

"I'll just put the milk on to heat for the chocolate," she said, and before Lacy could protest, swept into the kitchen through the newly built archway. Slater had obviously improved on the old home's architectural lines. Kaley approved.

The centerpiece of the kitchen was an old dinosaur of a wood-burning stove. Dirty tin plates and pots were piled into an old-fashioned sink not unlike her own. Soup cans and other debris spilled out of a trash bin. Even the shiny new refrigerator was stained with an array of fingerprints. One wall was lined with shelves on which canned goods and tools were haphazardly aligned.

"It's Lacy's turn to do dishes, but she won't," Jason said.

Kaley glanced at the girl. "I don't blame you. I'll bet you didn't *make* this mess."

Lacy stood stolid and sullen, ignoring the attempt at female camaraderie. Kaley paused. She wasn't about to leave the house until she'd seen Slater. "I have a few minutes to spare," she said casually. "So, why don't I just clear up this mess while the milk is heating."

"You have to heat dishwater in the kettle," Lacy volunteered, softening, but not much. "The hot-water tank isn't hooked up yet."

Kaley nodded. "I still do that at my house," she said agreeably. She shucked her hat and jacket, exchanging them for Slater's flannel shirt, which was hanging on the back of a chair. Fashioning it into an apron of sorts, she tied it about her waist.

"That's a pretty sweater," Lacy said, sounding as if the words were acrid on her tongue.

It was Kaley's best angora. "When you get a little bigger, you can borrow it," she offered.

"We won't be here when I get bigger. We're going to live with our mother."

"I'm not," said Jason. "I don't know her. I'm going to stay here and live with Uncle Slater and Aunt Willie. But I might go to heaven to see Daddy."

"You can't go to heaven, stupid. You have to be dead first. I told you."

Kaley kept quiet. She didn't quite know best how to intervene in the children's argument. Or even if she should.

"When is your mother coming?" she asked, and offhandedly began clearing the table.

"Christmas," Lacy said.

"That's what you said last Christmas," Jason reminded. "She didn't come."

"That's because she had a fight with Daddy on the phone. She will this year for sure. We're her kids and she has to take care of us."

Kaley heard the desperation and hope seep out between the child's words, and began to get a glimmer of the emotional turmoil that underlined Lacy's attitude.

"There," she said, wiping up food crumbs from the tabletop. "Now you have enough room to carve out your pumpkins."

Jason's face broke into a grin. "You mean I'm gonna get to cut out a face? With a knife? This is going to be the best Halloween I ever had!"

"If you're careful," Kaley told him. She went to retrieve the box she'd put in front of the hearth. Lacy followed like a sentry. "Why don't you add a log to the fire," Kaley suggested, hoping for a surreptitious moment to learn behind which door Slater lay ill or sleeping. Three doors led off the living area, one of which was slightly ajar. She felt a peculiar despair. She was torn between the desire to burst through each door and not wanting to add fuel to Lacy's hostility.

"Uncle Slater said we're not supposed to. We might burn down the house."

"Then you take the box into the kitchen while I do it."

"You're just here because Uncle Slater kissed you. You don't really care about little kids."

Kaley's eyes locked with the intent way Lacy was looking at her. It was to be the truth or nothing for the child. There was more to Lacy's stare than rebellion. Kaley saw the seeds of envy. When, she wondered, had the girl last been hugged or been the recipient of physical affection? She ached to take the child in her arms and smooth back the strands of hair that fell over her eyes.

"It's true I like your Uncle Slater," she said, replying to the accusation calmly. "But I also like little kids. I hope one day to have children of my own. I wish I already did. I wish I had a little girl." She stopped short of saying "one just like you."

Suspicion joined Lacy's deepening frown. "Why a little girl?"

Kaley said wistfully, "Probably because I want to be a better mother to her than my own mother was...is to me." She watched Lacy wrestle with that.

"Is your mother mean? Did she run off with a man?"

"No, she's very nice, just self-centered. She loves me, but not how I want to be loved. Or need to be loved."

"Can't you tell her?"

Kaley made a face of mock horror. "I wouldn't dare."

But Lacy wasn't buying it. "You're a grown-up. You can do anything you want."

"I can't. A grown-up knows all the rules and has no excuse not to follow them."

Lacy sucked in her narrow little cheeks. "Rules are harder for kids because grown-ups make them. If I was making rules, I'd make them easy."

"Well, make some then."

"Nobody would do what I said."

"You would. That's all the counts."

A bedspring squeaked and then a muffled groan emitted from behind the door that was slightly ajar. Kaley wanted to race toward the sound, but she restrained herself and only looked toward it.

Lacy grabbed her arm. "We better get back to Jason before he makes a big mess."

"Wait a minute, Lacy. Don't you think we ought to check on your uncle. He sounds ill."

"He'll be all right," the child said cavalierly. "He's had these spells before."

A chill raced down Kaley's spine. "I think I'd better look in on him."

Fear raced briefly across Lacy's face. She threw out her arms to block Kaley's passage. "No! He said not to bother him."

Kaley took the girl's hands firmly into her own. "I'm going in there. What's to be afraid of?" She was asking the question of herself as much as she was of Lacy.

Lacy nailed her with a look that Kaley read as, "you tricked me, you're one of them!" and jerked her hands free. "Do it, then!" she cried. "I don't care!" She ran out of the room as if she'd been fired from a cannon.

Chapter Six

The room was dark. Kaley felt for the light switch. Finding only capped wire stubs, she stood on the threshold allowing her eyes to adjust to night vision. Here, too, were the smells of sawdust and raw lumber and kerosene.

Slowly the room took shape. It was large and square, and centered against one wall was a huge modern bed within which she could make out Slater's bulk. A solid chair served as a nightstand. Upon it was an old hurricane lamp, a necessary standby against winter storms for those who lived in the upper reaches of Fentress County.

Slater's breathing was steady but stentorian.

She glided into the room quietly, felt about for matches on the chair seat and, removing the lamp's chimney, lighted the wick.

Now she could see that the room spread out and away to a row of long windows that during the summer would allow indoors the filigreed light of the staunch old oak at the side of the house.

It was destined to be a grand and masculine room, sized for a man of Slater's length and breadth.

"Too bright," he said, his voice low and hoarse.

Kaley whirled, startled to see him regarding her with burning eyes. At once she adjusted the wick until only a soft arc of pewter colored them both.

He was tucked inside a well-worn sleeping bag, his long, somewhat curly hair splayed over a pillow. Beard stubble outlined his rough-hewn jaw. What scared her were the deep stamped lines about his mouth and the gauntness of a face clutched by pain.

"What's wrong with you?"

"Headache."

"A headache can slay an Argonaut? I don't believe you." She sat beside him on the bed and laid a hand on his brow.

"More than a headache, Slater. You've a fever. Have you been bathing in that icy creek and caught pneumonia?"

"A good sleep is all I need," he said on an exhaled breath. He turned back a fold of the sleeping bag, revealing a swath of his broad chest. "Wanna crawl in here and cozy up?"

"This is no time for wit. You're really sick."

"Cozying up is witty? I'm out of touch."

"You are. However irate they become, men don't go around tossing women over their shoulders these days."

"Had to get your attention."

"I much prefer the way you have of showing me up a liar."

"Bad form to do that twice, missy."

"We can argue that point when you're better able to hold up your end."

A band of pain circled his head, gripping like a vise. He wrenched out a question. "What...brought...you here?"

"I had some Halloween treats for Lacy and Jason."

"Treats." And after a moment, "What for me? Tricks?"

"Pie and homemade pumpkin brandy."

"I'm having delirious dreams," he said, closing his eyes.

A silence came down between them. Somewhere in the room a clock ticked. A windup clock, Kaley surmised, because the rhythmic ticking was unsteady. "Or maybe it's my own heart," she murmured to herself, as if that explained it.

The sound of her voice did not arouse Slater. She watched his lids flutter, but his eyes stayed closed. His lashes were long and thick and lay on a face drained of color.

She sat there while he fell into a thin sleep. A part of her wanted to race for help; another part was content to study him without having to be coy or ill-mannered about it. The soft swell of joy that lifted her heart astounded her.

It was true, then. There was such a thing as love at first sight. At first glimpse. Instant romance. In college she had always been odd girl out, taking forever to decide if she liked a boy or not, by which time he was long gone. She had dated Virgil off and on for two years before she became serious.

Her first glimpse of Slater and she'd gone bonkers. She offered up a silent apology to her college roommate who came back to the dorm from every other date madly in love. Kaley had teased her: "Madly in lust, you mean."

Serves me right, Kaley mused, veering away from introspection as Slater stretched and turned on his side.

"You smell wonderful," he mumbled. "Like the Tea and Sugar. Ought to stop and make camp, missy. Dust storm comin'."

He's had these spells before.

She shook him awake. "Do you have medicine you take? Where is it?"

When it became obvious he wasn't going to answer, her eyes swept the room, resting finally on a small, elaborately carved wooden chest. She carried it over to the chair and began to rummage in it. She found his passport, a packet of letters tied with a string that bore an Atlanta, Georgia, return address from Wilhelmina Rutledge, a chamois of rocks and colored stones, postcards depicting Australian scenes, maps, a leather folder, photographs—nothing that resembled medication of any sort.

Frustrated, she closed the box and shoved it beneath the bed.

"...smell...like cinnamon."

"Slater, can you hear me? I'm going to call Jessie."

There were no covers to adjust, no way to make Slater more comfortable, zippered as he was into the sleeping bag. Needing to touch him, she brushed hair off his brow and touched her fingertip to his eyelids.

"I'll be back in a moment," she whispered. "Can you sleep a little?"

"Watch out for Jerome," he muttered. "He'll clip your wings."

There seemed to be an invisible cloth of urgency smothering her as she made the hot chocolate for the children and set the basket of cookies before them. All of which she did to the thrumming of Lacy's hostility. The girl sat on the floor with her back against the wall, watching. "We can have all we want?" Jason asked, eyes saucer-wide.

"As long as you don't eat so fast you become ill, too," Kaley cautioned. "I'm going to call my friend, Jessie, the nurse you met at my house, to come see your uncle."

Lacy's head came up sharply, looking at Kaley with a wisdom left over from some other life, which muted her hostility a little. "Will she take him away?"

"We don't want to go to a foster home and be separated because we're orphans," said Jason around a mouthful of cookie.

Kaley was appalled. "Of course you won't go to a foster home. Whatever put that idea in your head?"

"Aunt Willie said. If Uncle Slater didn't take care of us, that's where we'd have to go."

"But not if our mother got here in time," Lacy injected.

"If Slater has to go into the hospital, the both of you can stay with me until he comes home. You won't have to go anywhere else or be separated." She smiled purposefully. "But I don't think it will come to that. He only has a fever. Where's your telephone?"

Lacy pointed to the kitchen shelves.

It was still in its box. Kaley's heart sank. "The lines aren't up yet?"

The girl shook her head.

"WHATEVER IT IS you want, Kaley, the answer is no," Jessie said into the receiver once Kaley had identified herself. "It's Saturday night, I've got a date, his wife left him and took the dog. It's the dog he misses. Opportunity is knocking and I'm opening—"

"Slater's sick. He's got a fever, maybe pneumonia—he's the color of putty. You've got to come. I'm at my place now, but I'm going back. Tell me what to do until you get there. Jessie—he looks *awful.*" Kaley's deep cavity of fear projected itself over the wires. "He could die while we're talking. The children are up there, alone with him. I have to get back right away."

Jessie sighed heavily. "What I won't do for a friend."

"Thank you," Kaley breathed.

"How high is the fever?"

"I don't know. High."

"Was he conscious?"

"Yes—but talking out of it a bit."

"Did you give him anything? Aspirin? Soup?"

"Nothing—I was scared to."

"All right, it'll take me at least an hour, though. Lucky you, I had the snow chains put on my car this afternoon."

It was the longest hour in Kaley's recent memory. She returned to the Rutledge homestead with quilts and basins and towels and anything else she could think of that might be of some use. Still, she felt helpless.

Slater lay on his bed like a felled tree. She allowed the children to carve the pumpkins, then heated water for their baths and helped Jason into his pajamas.

Lacy refused her efforts.

Resigned and absorbed in her own anguish, Kaley suggested the girl sit with her uncle while she put Jason to bed.

She was amazed by the ritual required to settle him on one of the obviously new twin beds.

"Garfield goes here and Snoozy by me and all my Ninja Turtles go there," he informed, pointing toward his feet. "Else they get under my back when I sleep and hurt."

"There won't be any room for you."

"Yes, there is. See?" He crawled in from the top and slid down between his stuffed toys. Kaley kissed him on his brow.

"The cookies were good," he said.

"I'll make you some more soon."

"You could put M&M's on top. I love M&M's."

"I'll do that," she said, with a strained smile.

"Don't turn off the light," he called, alarmed, when her hand was on the switch. "I don't want the angels of mercy to come and get me like they did Daddy. They took him away, y'know, and he isn't allowed back. Not even to see me."

Kaley drew her smile and breath simultaneously. "The angels of mercy came and got my husband, too. His name was Virgil. So, I know how it is."

"Have they let him come see you?" he asked in a sibilant whisper, as if fearful the walls had ears, or that the angels might be only around the corner.

"No, they haven't."

He sighed. "Mean old things. Just like Lacy sometimes." He turned away from her then and, nuzzling into the teddy bear, began to suck his thumb.

With varying degrees of despair for company, Kaley returned to Slater's room.

Lacy was curled up at the foot of his bed, soundly asleep. Kaley covered her with a quilt. The thin and angular features of the child were softened in sleep to a sweetness that belied her hardscrabble attitude.

Slater, too, appeared to sleep.

There was nothing more for her to do except keep company with the silence of the house. In the front room she built up the fire in the hearth and sat on the floor before it, arms wrapped about her knees, head cocked listening for Jessie. She willed herself not to pray, because that would be admitting Slater might truly be as badly off as she had indicated to Jessie.

The nurse arrived with a squeal of brakes, snow chains rattling and, dressed to the nines.

"I hate it that I had to pull you away from a fun evening," Kaley offered.

"Count it as a Halloween trick. I'll think up a whopper of one for you next year. Count on it. Where is he?"

After Kaley directed her to Slater's inert form, Jessie smiled. "Nah, maybe this'll be a treat, after all." She spied the bundle that was Lacy. "Good grief, Kaley. Get that child out of here. Suppose he's contagious."

"Sorry. She fell asleep there. I wasn't thinking." Lacy was all thin arms and legs, heavier in slumber than Kaley anticipated, but she didn't awaken as Kaley carried her across the house and made her snug in the twin bed opposite Jason's.

When she returned to Slater's room, he was drowsily awake and he and Jessie were arguing.

"Here's the way it is, big fella," Jessie was saying. "I gave up a high old time to come up here and be a ministering angel. Now, this thermometer goes under your tongue or up your kazoo. Either way suits me."

"I'd like to see you try putting anything up *my* kazoo, missy."

"I get all kinds of threats," Jessie told him airily. "Mostly from men who don't have on clean underwear."

"Not my excuse. I'm not wearing any."

Jessie grinned. "Then why don't you just be a good boy and put this under your tongue," she cajoled. "Do it as a favor to Kaley. She can return the favor later."

Moving his head only a fraction, he shifted his gaze, impaling Kaley with an obdurate stare. "Put like that, how can I refuse?"

For all the time he tolerated Jessie taking his pulse, listening to his chest, indicating for him to sit up, which he did, wincing and holding his neck stiff, his gaze was locked onto Kaley like a vise. Jessie listened to his lungs, and thumped him on his broad back and looked into his ears. He didn't break the lock on Kaley until Jessie lifted his lids and flashed a light into his eyes.

"Mmmph," she said.

He spit the thermometer out. "That's your diagnosis?" She'd never be able to discern the real problem he had. That had taken CAT scans and X rays and half a dozen Australian specialists, confirmed by their counterparts in Atlanta.

"The fever indicates an infection somewhere, dear heart," she said retrieving the thermometer from the folds of the sleeping bag, reading it and making notes in her little notebook. "Your heart is beating steady as a drum and your lungs are clear, so we can rule out pneumonia. Suppose I just take a little of your blood and let the lab techs figure it."

"I much prefer to keep what blood I have, missy."

Standing against the wall, arms crossed watching anxiously, Kaley felt a stab of jealousy. She didn't like him calling Jessie missy. She'd gotten used to him calling her that, like an endearment, sort of.

Jessie took his blood pressure, then tied the rubber band about his biceps—the one with the wild stallion tattoo—to bring up a vein from which to draw his blood. Slater flexed his muscles. The rubber band popped loose.

"All right, Hercules," Jessie said, smiling sweetly at him. "I get your message. Here's mine. A doctor I'm not, but I do have the authority to quarantine you."

"Wouldn't honor it," he said.

"Have you arrested," she said.

"Take the bloody stuff then."

She did and, after labeling it, dispatched the vial into her bag with quick efficiency.

"Best I can tell, outside the fever, you're fine. You can have juice, tea, whatever you'll eat." She stood up, taking in both Kaley and Slater. "You *are* quarantined, until the report comes back from the lab. Monday afternoon probably. I'll alert Miss Broom why the kids won't be in school."

"What the hell..." sputtered Slater, rising from his pillow.

"I mean it," she warned. "You're recently here from a foreign country. The wilds of that country, from the stories you told at supper that night at Kaley's. You could be incubating a disease, carrying anything from dengue fever to the plague. I just want you to stay put as a precaution."

"But, why me?" Kaley protested. "I still have orders to fill. I have to get them sent off Monday morning."

"I've been vaccinated against everything! All I've got is a damned headache," Slater growled. "And I know the reason for it, even if you don't. It's not contagious."

Both women looked at him. Kaley asked, "What reason?"

"None of your damned business, missy."

Jessie arched an eyebrow. "Suit yourself." To Kaley she said, "You're quarantined—you've been in close contact with Slater. Isn't that his shirt wrapped around your waist?"

"You've been in contact with him!"

"Wonderful logic, Kaley, but I'm the visiting nurse. I know how to protect myself. I'll stop by and leave a message for Independent so he'll know where you are."

"You mean I can't even *go home?*"

"For all his spit and sputter, Independent is an old man. You know he's never had so much as measles or a polio vaccine."

Kaley looked from Jessie to Slater and back to Jessie. "We're friends. Can't you make an exception? I won't go near Independent And look at Slater. He's sitting up. He's better already."

"Fentress County can't afford an epidemic, Kaley. And I wouldn't want to be the one responsible, if it came to that."

Kaley turned on Slater. "You better have nothing worse than the ague or the flu!" she said, angry in her fear and dismay.

"All I've got is a bloody headache! If you hadn't invited yourself up here and gone hysterical, I'd still be sleeping it away."

"Oh, so now it's all my fault."

Jessie snapped her bag closed. "Well, I'll leave you two to sort it out. I'll hurry the lab techs and be back Monday afternoon the latest."

Kaley trailed Jessie to her car. "That was a sham show for Slater's benefit, wasn't it? Trick or treat? We aren't really quarantined."

Jessie tilted her head, smiling. "I could've called it either way. Look at it this way, you've had no previous experience with a man even remotely like Slater.

You might learn whether he's worth agonizing over or not.''

''I haven't been agonizing!''

''Well, what do you call it?''

''So, I can go home?''

''Nope.'' Jessie sobered. ''I meant what I said. There is the possibility, however remote, that Slater is carrying something contagious. I suspect that fever is chronic. Won't hurt to find out why. If you prefer, I will telephone for an ambulance and have him hauled into the isolation ward at the hospital until Monday.''

''*I prefer?* You decide. He'd never forgive me!''

''I have decided,'' Jessie reminded. ''Now, go back in there and tend to the poor fellow before you catch pneumonia. Loneliness is a potent illness, too, y'know.''

''He's not lonely.''

''I didn't mean him. Bye now.''

''Jessie! Come back! You can't. . .''

But Jessie had her windows rolled up and motor revving, her attention on backing up onto the snow-covered lane.

Feeling light-headed and weightless, her heart thudding like a trapped bird, Kaley returned to Slater's house and sat cross-legged before the dwindling fire, her mind going six ways to a dozen.

One thought rose to the surface. *Trapped.* And she'd done it to herself.

''Have to hand it to you, missy, you set that up neat as a pin. Couldn't have done better had I plotted it myself.''

Kaley scrambled to her feet. Slater had donned jeans and socks. His hair fell unkempt to his shoulders, the effect being to enhance his wide shoulders, draw attention to his chest and how well he filled out the jeans.

"I'm as upset as you are, but I didn't plot anything. Jessie takes her job seriously. I know that. Had I thought it out, I wouldn't have called her. I got scared."

"For me?"

Kaley dissembled. "You were faking, weren't you? You don't look ill at all now."

"I had a headache. It comes and goes."

"It's gone?"

"It's bearable."

"Are you going to honor the quarantine?"

"As it happens, I don't have any plans the next few days outside of working here. I'll have the kids home from school on Monday. No big deal."

"I think I'll go along home."

"Do that," he said. *Go home before I close the distance between us and put you in my house, in my bed and in my heart until death do us part, or what will pass for death when I'm doddering around with no sense of who you are. Or who I am.*

Kaley sniffled unhappily. "Don't rush me!"

"I was only being agreeable. But we both know you're not going to set foot out that door until Jessie releases us."

"Sure I will."

"You won't. You're the kind of person who'll stop for a red light in the middle of nowhere and no oncoming traffic for miles around. In other words, missy, you're the kind of woman who follows the rules, however silly they are." He tilted his head. "Which is a good thing, because I have a few rules of my own."

"What kind of rules?"

"Telling wouldn't be any fun. I'll let you know when you break one."

"What good will that do?"

"So I can collect the fine." He stepped up to her and began untying his shirt from her waist. "You don't mind do you? Hate to put on a clean one so late in the day."

She brushed his hands away. A sick and weakened Slater flat on his back was one thing. A healthy, viable, teasing and testing Slater was quite another. "You only had to ask," she said, unwrapping the shirt from her waist and handing it to him.

He held it to his face and sniffed. "Very nice," he murmured.

Kaley felt like a balloon a week after the party. "Flirting isn't going to get you anywhere, Slater, so stop it. For all I know, you might have some horrible social disease."

He looked at her blankly for a heartbeat, then clarity struck and he laughed. "Oh, missy, love...the only thing wrong with me is entirely socially acceptable—to everyone but me. Had I what you're thinking, I'd have kelley'd up out in the bush alone until an aborigine spirit man came along and pronounced me dead."

"Then what causes your headaches?" she asked, abashed only a little because her curiosity was aroused.

"Busybodies like you."

He turned and ambled into the kitchen. Kaley followed hesitantly because she didn't know what was required of her now that the patient was up and about.

Slater was filling a pot with water. "I'll brew us a cup of tea," he said. "Got used to it in the bush. Can't seem to go an evening without it now."

The children had made a glorious mess with the pumpkin carving. Seeds and stringy wet membrane and bits of pumpkin were everywhere. Across the room, looking not exactly fit, but strong and virile, Slater brewed tea. "You know what I feel like?" she fumed. "Like I've walked into one play while having learned the lines for another."

"Understandable, missy. You like things predictable. It shows."

"If I liked things predictable, I certainly wouldn't like you," she said, at the tail end of her composure.

"Clean us off a bit of that table, love. We'll talk about it."

With faltering grace, Kaley scraped the seeds and scraps into a bucket, then took a swipe at the table with a rag. She rinsed it at the sink. Slater bagged her there.

He gazed down at her, then lifted a length of her hair to his nose. "Cinnamon. You've been cooking with it."

"In the pumpkin nut bread," she said, and skittered away from his nearness, disparaging her own cowardice. After all, wanting to be near him was why she was here at all.

"Pumpkin nut bread. That'll make for a proper tea." He indicated a knife and a pair of tin plates on the shelf for her to slice and serve the bread.

The tea, brewed to the color of tar, was also served in tin mugs. Slater heaped sugar into his.

"Rot your teeth," she admonished perversely. "What's 'the tea and sugar'?"

"A train, a shopping center on rails. Crosses South Australia into Western Australia once a week. Buy your groceries off it."

She wrapped her hands around the tin cup, warming them. "You miss the life you led there, don't you?"

He sipped his tea. "The cities are like any other metropolis. It's the bush country that tests a man's mettle."

"You went there to test yourself?"

"Not at first, but that's what happens. It's the kind of country that'll bring out the best or the worst in a man."

"Which did it bring out in you?"

His reply came with the barest hint of a smile. "It got me both sides."

Kaley lifted an eyebrow. "Which side is sitting across from me right now?"

He grinned. "My wicked side."

A sudden animation strummed within her. To cover it, she sipped the tea and found it awful.

"Good?" he asked.

"Terrific," she equivocated.

He tilted his chair back, spoke softly. "So you like me, missy?"

Kaley plucked at a nonexistent thread on her sweater. *Go ahead,* an inner voice coaxed, *give it your best shot.* "Actually, I do."

His laughter was muted. "Actually."

Her eyes snapped up to his face. "Improbable as it may seem . . ."

"I like you liking me," he said affably. It felt good, but the kernel of dread that was ever within him seemed to expand. Somewhere down the not too distant road he expected to lose his sight, his mobility. Some of it anyway. Who knew how the damned thing growing inside his skull would affect him. All he'd gotten was a long list of probables. "Have to tell you up front, though, that if this is a ploy to work Rutledge land—"

"It isn't! Come spring, I'll harvest farther afield. There are other mountains around here and I'm certain I can get whatever leases or cooperation I need from the owners."

"And are we cooking up long-range plans?"

Kaley sniffed. Of course she was. "The only thing I've cooked is cookies, nut bread and pumpkin pie—Oh! I left the pie in the truck. It's probably frozen solid by now," she wailed, pushing back her chair.

Slater stopped her with a raised hand. "In that case, it'll keep."

"But—"

"Not the time for you to skitter off, missy. Conversation is just getting interesting. Don't you want to know if I like you?"

Kaley felt her stomach twist. She must've nodded because he went on.

"Matter of fact, the instant I see you, I get this compulsion to start peeling off my clothes. Most times, that would be embarrassing." Watching her very carefully, trying to look past the dazed expression in her eyes, he reached across the table and took her hands in his. "This isn't one of those times."

Kaley was thinking how he could easily encircle her waist with his hands, and she had to fight hard to hear what he was saying. Finally it occurred to her what he was suggesting.

"You don't expect me to stand up do you?" she said over the clatter of her heart and a peculiar airy sensation in her midsection. "It's my knees. They've gone all . . . numb."

He came around the table and scooped her up into his arms. "What I have in mind doesn't require standing."

"Not again! Slater, put me down. You're weak—"

"Who said?"

"But, you are."

"Weak in the head, perhaps. The rest of me is prime. You're the one with the problem knees. Now, if I can just find a place to put you down so I can have a look at them—" He nuzzled her ear as he carried her into his room.

Kaley put her arms around his neck and nestled her head in the space between his shoulder and his ear. "We ought not," she murmured. "You're sick. You feel awfully warm."

"I *am* awfully warm, missy."

Chapter Seven

Inside the bedroom, the glow of the kerosene lantern was soothing after the glaring overhead bulb in the kitchen.

Kaley burned with a mixture of terror and exhilaration. Somewhere on the far side of her brain a voice sent out a caution. Did she want him to know and explore all of her secret longings? To allow such intimacy was an avowal of faith and trust far beyond mere friendship or lust. To give herself so entirely to Slater was scary. And yet—she could not imagine life without him.

Not for anything was she going to allow common sense and reality to intrude.

Slater deposited her on his bed into the imprint he'd left earlier. That was as it should be, Kaley thought, and her arms tightened about his neck so that he was obliged to lie down beside her. He exuded sensuousness as strong as animal musk. She inhaled deeply.

"Some neighbor you turned out to be," she said softly, shifting her body so that more of her met more of him.

"Is that a complaint?"

"Far from it, you goose."

"You feel the chill?"

"Not a bit." How could she, snug in his powerful arms? "You?"

"I'm a bloody bonfire, missy." To prove it, his hand slipped underneath her sweater. The sensation of his warm palm, rough against her skin, caused her breasts to stretch tight, her nipples to swell.

Her fingertip traced the scar amid the hair on his chest. "How did you get this?"

"A fight."

"I can't imagine you losing a fight."

"Didn't," he replied, voice tight with ardor. "Got careless."

She lifted up slightly so that she could study his face; the strong cheekbones, the rugged square chin softened somewhat now by beard stubble. She touched his mouth, running a finger along his lower lip. "You have an expressive mouth, Slater. Did you know that when you smile, one corner crinkles up?"

His hands slid down to her waist, began unzipping her slacks. "Let me guess," he murmured into her hair, "you're one of those women who talk all through sex."

"One of *those* women?"

"Never mind, they didn't have faces." His hands moved inside her waistband to cup the smooth flesh of her derriere. A moan of pleasure erupted from him.

"I have a face, a name—if that's what this is going to..."

"Beautiful face," he said, drawing her close, nuzzling the soft flesh under her jawbone. "Funny face." He nipped her chin with his teeth. "Nice face..."

"Won't be a nice face if you keep rubbing your beard on it," she said thickly because his hands were busy, shoving her slacks down over her hips, catching them with his foot to move them down her legs. She kicked off her shoes and the unwanted tethering was flung to the floor.

"I'll shave," he said, pushing away from her and smiling.

She pulled him back. "Tomorrow."

He smiled. "Bloody right, missy. I'm not getting out of this bed—not now."

She felt his hand between them, at his waist, unzipping his jeans.

"Let me," she whispered, putting her hands on his.

"Careful," he warned, but she had no need of warnings. He was free—hard and hot and smooth—a magnet for her fingers.

Slater gasped at her tentative touch.

"That feel good, Slater?"

"Witch," he said on an exhaled breath. It was as though her fingertips were playing an erotic melody upon him, matching beat for throbbing beat. He could feel himself growing more tumescent. The pleasure was exquisite to the point of pain.

Continuing the melody, Kaley lowered her hand to lift the weight that made him the man he was. Her touch was no more than a feather stroke.

Slater held his breath.

"What about this, hmm?" She bent her head and took his nipple into her mouth.

Beset by sensations that heretofore had existed only in his imagination, Slater had no voice.

His roaming hands encountered the fabric of her sweater. "This has to come off," he said, spewing the wire-taut words as if they'd be the last he'd ever speak.

Kaley lifted her head. "An oversight soon remedied." She scrambled to her knees and tugged the offending garment over her head.

For a moment she was mere shadow poised on her knees upon the bed. Then the flickering lantern light caught her in its glow. Her hair was an extraordinary rippling mane of amber, falling around her shoulders. Her breasts were full with passion, nipples erect; her waist was so slim Slater knew he could span it with his hands. Her hips curved outward to flow into creamy thighs; an ethereal goddess come to life, he thought, mesmerized. Of course, he was still caught up in a feverish dream. That explained it. Then she spoke.

"Slater?" Hesitant.

"I'm listening." He was afraid to reach for her should she prove to be a dream when he touched her.

"You're staring at me. Are you finding warts or something?"

He gave a small burst of soft laughter. She was as real and solid as the walls that kept the wailing wind at bay. "You're beyond perfection, love. No warts." He reached out, touched her throat, drawing his fingers down between her breasts, to her navel. "I'm going to possess you... absorb you..." The yearning in his voice sounded physical, as if it lived on its own, a separate being in his chest.

She made as if to lie down beside him again. "No. Stay there," he commanded, his hand spanning her abdomen to push her gently back until her buttocks were resting on her heels.

He stroked her body, first along the hip, then onward to the silky junction of her thighs. Exploring with his hand, he felt the softness between her legs.

Kaley stiffened.

His hand stilled. "No?"

"Yes," she whispered.

Slater paused, gazing at her face. He knew instinctively that she was offering him the gift of herself, completely, wholly, nothing withheld. He went gently, almost reverently.

Beneath his fingers, her flesh grew damp; he felt her blossom and swell. She arched her back, reaching toward his hand with her hips.

And this is only the beginning, he thought.

Her shoulders were lovely. He ran his tongue over her collarbone, planting kisses in the throbbing hollows of her neck. Touching his tongue to a pulsating vein, and feeling the force of life as it flowed within her, caused him to think he was learning a new and exotic language.

When his hand moved from between her legs to cup her breast and pearl its nipple, her hips lunged after him in protest.

"We'll get back there again, missy."

"Soon?" she moaned, feeling herself so fulsome with the ache of desire she was reminded of a water-filled balloon stretched to bursting.

"Not too soon, my darling. There's this..." Drawing her down into his arms, he took a proprietary interest in an erect nipple; he covered it with his mouth and sucked.

Kaley became aware of every ounce of blood boiling within her. It roared through her ears, spilling down her neck to splash in great waves into her heart only to race away again, pumping and pulsing, mimicking the rhythm of Slater's tongue on the tender erect tip of her nipple.

It came to her, when she could manage a thought, that she could provide him with the same soaring pleasure that he was bestowing on her. Her hand searched him out again and curled around his sex. He shifted his weight to accommodate her, but when her fingers began to pump and pulse from groin to tip, he cried out.

"Whoa!" He stopped her, locking her hands above her head.

"Let me," she pleaded, squirming against him.

"Can't, missy. You'll turn this into a slam-bam-thank-you-ma'am."

"Then what am I to do?" she wailed in a whisper.

"Let me make love to you."

"I want to make love back. You're asking me to just lie here like a limp rag."

"Hardly limp," he said, flicking one of her erect nipples with his tongue.

"Slater..." she ground out, trying to pull her hands free.

"Shh," he said, and to get his way, devoured her mouth, kissing away her protest.

She fought for release but he held her hands firm and draped a powerful leg across her knees. Captured, she could only submit. As soon as she surrendered to one sensation, another evolved and took its place.

He stroked her body with hand and tongue, his erection pulsating against her; at times tantalizingly near her soft inner thighs, at others, probing her concave abdomen.

Finally, her nerves stretched to the delicious extremity of pleasure, she wrested her mouth from his. "You're not being fair, Slater."

He began nibbling on her ear. "What do you know about being fair, my sweet. You served me dinner with your shirt unbuttoned down to your navel."

"Not true. Two buttons from the top—that's all."

"Two or ten, the results were the same. Had me slavering like a dingo in heat, and left me sleepless with only erotic dreams for company."

"Turn loose my hands. Please. I want to touch you, to know you the way you're knowing me."

He kissed her eyelids, the tip of her nose. "You want to besot me, make me helpless."

"No more than you're making me," she said, bemused, accepting the fact that she was going crazy, if not in fact already there.

He kissed the soft inner flesh of her elbows.

"We'll rest a moment," he said thickly. "Count this as a kindness." Hc released her hands; freed himself, he rested his head on the palm of one hand and studied her while the other traveled, recording the delicious smoothness of her skin. "You glow as if sprinkled with fairy dust," he said.

"I am glowing, darling. I've never felt so aglow in my life. You make me feel special. I don't believe I've ever met anyone quite like you—ever."

"An exaggeration," he countered lazily, but her avowal reached deep within him, attaching itself to his sinewy tendons, lodging there for life. He liked being special to someone. It was the highest compliment she could've conferred upon him.

Jerome had been the high achiever in the family. It had been impossible to get out from beneath his brother's shadow—until he'd gone to Australia. His adventures and deeds there were the daily happenstance lived by any bushman toughened by the harsh landscape.

Kaley felt like mewing as she curled against him. "There's not one whit of exaggeration in what I say. Give me a minute to catch my breath and I'll see if I can find a way to convince you."

Her smell on him, the taste of her on his lips, were the emotional quotient of earth and fire. "There's nothing like the explosion of passion to make a woman eloquent," he said, submerging his tumbling emotions.

"Eloquent?" Kaley laughed softly. "Slater, I may glow with fairy dust, but I feel positively vulgar. I couldn't manage eloquence if it was stuffed in my apron pocket. But I can manage this,'' she crooned, as hands began anew to seek him out with impish delight.

Her fingers stroked the swollen tip of his manhood.

Slater groaned. ''You never learn, do you, missy?'' He seized her hands, locking them once more above her head as he mounted her, spreading her legs with his knee.

His heavy, pulsating sex touched her where she was moist and urgently warm; her muscles contracted of their own volition.

He gyrated his hips slowly, exploring the threshold, anticipating his welcome, not thrusting, but poised, absorbing each sensation fed into his brain by his sensitive, exploring erection.

Kaley arched her hips toward him, reaching for him, breathlessly anticipating the first glorious thrust; for a heartbeat she was frightened. But no. She was wet with desire, ready for him.

Above her, Slater hung motionless. He seemed not to have moved for an eon. Looking up into his face, she tried to pull her hands free.

''Slater?''

His eyes, lids at halfmast, met hers; yet he wasn't seeing her. She could tell. He was gazing inward, unaware of the expression of utter bleakness that robbed his face of vitality.

''What is it?'' Dread cloaked the question lightly, though she felt it clear to her bone marrow.

''I can't do this, missy.''

Can't! She lay there stunned. "But—it's so right. Oh, darling... your headache. It's worsened?"

He rolled away and sprawled on the bed, managing not to touch her at any point. "My headache's gone."

"Then—" she stammered, at a loss for words. Every pore in her body screamed for sexual release. Bewildered, she sat up. "Did I do something wrong? Say something that turned you off? You men are such finicky creatures, especially in bed."

"You did nothing wrong. You're perfect." He expelled a breath more groan than sigh.

"You stopped out of guilt. You didn't mean a single thing you said."

"I meant every word."

In her mind, Kaley ticked off other explanations for his stopping.

He didn't like her.

Yes, he did. And with every pound of flesh he owned. A woman knew. *She* knew.

She had been too brash and forward. Maybe.

One reason rose glaringly to the surface. She gasped.

"You're gay, aren't you. That's why you couldn't put... that's why you went to Australia. You hide it behind brawn and tattoos. You went to Australia to test your masculinity."

Slater's mouth dropped open before he caught himself. Then he laughed. Crooking his elbow over his eyes, he kept on laughing. His laughter reverberated off the walls.

"Stop!" Kaley said, delivering the plea in an angry, sibilant hiss. "You'll wake Lacy and Jason." She yanked his elbow down. "Okay. You're not gay. You hate women."

"I adore women. I adore you. That's it, you see."

She stiffened, a naked virago ready to do battle. "That's the most convoluted backpedaling I've ever heard. I *don't* see."

He reached for the bed covers, chancing upon the quilt Kaley had used to cover Lacy. "Where'd this come from?"

"I brought it."

He covered her with it, wrapping her shoulders, overlapping the quilt from neck to knee.

"Out of sight, out of mind?" she said with arctic civility, using sarcasm to submerge the agony of desire that clung to every cell in her body.

"No. I wish I could explain, but I can't."

"Try," she said, softening to a degree.

He gazed into the cavernous overhead shadows where thick support beams were barely visible. Kaley had been more accurate than she knew, he thought ruefully. Out of sight and out of mind was the prognosis. It was all too easy for him to imagine himself shuffling about in his infirmity, blind, mindless and unaware of any beauty; a hulking shell of the man he was today.

Would someone as young and vibrant as Kaley Jackson want that kind of albatross in her life?

Had he possessed her with every fiber of his being, and he'd been on that track, he knew in his gut he'd never be able to be so unselfish to let her go.

"Come back from wherever you are," Kaley said, placing her hand lightly on his chest.

"It's still no good," he told her.

Kaley was still damp between her thighs, aching with the images of unrequited lovemaking. Her heart pounded sickly. "I never thought...I should never have come here."

"Not with this in mind, although, I'm glad you did. You're always welcome."

"You're such a smoothie, Slater, channeling all that arrogance and teasing into warmth—"

"The bane of my existence, missy."

"Stop calling me missy! You're laughing at me."

"You're talking willy-nilly. Shut up."

"I won't. You owe me an explanation."

"That's simple enough. I can't be a permanent fixture in your life."

Why not? "Did I ask you to be?"

"Give me credit, love. I know the difference between a quick lay and what was happening in this bed. What's been happening since the moment we laid eyes on each other. Cupid used an ax on us. Guess he figured that's what it'd take."

She was electrified into sudden immobility. It was a full minute before she could reply. "You're saying we've fallen in *love?*" she said, despairingly in need of confirmation.

"We've fallen into something."

Her heart lurched wildly. He was looking past her, detached, watching the play of light and shadow cast by the lantern. The shadows were lengthening as the wick burned itself out. The muscles in his biceps were bulging with tension. He wasn't as detached as he pretended. "Is being in love bad?" she asked, keeping her tone carefully bland.

"Not bad—useless." He didn't like slamming the door on himself or on her. God knows, he didn't have a clue as to how he'd be able to keep his hands off her. He wouldn't even consider chasing her from his thoughts. Even he knew some things were impossible. But this... He laughed at himself—after all his years of thumbing his nose at "the right thing to do," here he was about to preach it.

"I'm committed, Kaley. I've a pair of orphans in tow, a farm that's nothing but rock and shale, and an elderly, crippled aunt who's looking to me for salvation." His excuse was weak even to his own ears, but it was the best he could present.

Kaley dropped her head onto her knees. Dear God. Almost anything she said now would sound like begging. "But I want you so," she cried.

Though her words were muffled by the quilt, their impact was not lost on Slater. Covered with the sleeping bag, the true condition of his feelings were mirrored at the juncture of his thighs.

"The wanting would be worse later," he said, "because then we'd know."

"Damn you!" she cried, lifting her head. "Why did you start this?"

"Kaley, my love, I'm a man. I wanted you."

"And now you don't," she said flatly.

His vision blurred, a telltale reminder. When she came clearly into focus again, he said thickly, "I want you, but it won't work between us."

She stumbled off the bed, dragging the quilt. "I've made a fool of myself again. Where you're concerned I just can't seem to help myself."

"If it's any consolation, you're a beautiful fool."

"Fat lot of good that does," she railed, dismay and anger roiling within her. She turned and faced him, her eyes lighted with determination and flashing with fury. "I won't let you get away with this." She was holding the quilt in such a manner that the swell of her breasts erupted tantalizingly above the quilt edge, an unconscious emphasis to her resolution.

"We're extending our families' feud to our generation?"

"Feud?" Kaley laughed to keep from crying. "Slater, I'm going to drive you crazy, or...off this mountain and out of my life." She stormed around to his side of the bed accompanied by a wind that sang harsh whistling music at the edges of the windows. She stood over him in the waning arc of light. "Starting now."

She dropped the quilt, it puddled at her feet. "Look at me," she commanded, cupping her breasts in her hands. "You kissed these..."

"Kaley—don't."

Her hands trailed down her abdomen until her fingertips were at her silky divide. "And you touched me here."

Fascination reigned. Slater couldn't tear his eyes away.

Kaley spied her underpants caught on the corner of the small box she'd shoved under the bed. She bent forward, holding the pose a heartbeat so that he had a particularly captivating view of her bare breasts.

"You won't win," he ground out, covering his eyes with his arm to shut her out.

"If I don't, you don't," she whispered, bending closer to flick her tongue out to touch his earlobe.

"Stop that."

She smiled. "Slap my face, Slater." It was an echo.

His elbow came down, his eyes filling with consternation. "I don't hit women."

"Seems like you don't do anything else with them, either. Now, where's my sweater?"

"That's hitting below the belt."

"I know, darling. That's why I said it." Her hand slid alongside of him, searching, moving swiftly over his knees, then inside his thigh.

"For crying out loud," he croaked.

She let her hand brush his still-hard tumescense. He grabbed her wrist. "That's enough. No more games."

"It's your checkerboard, darling. You made the rules. It's not nice to change them when I'm winning."

"I concede defeat, now get your clothes on."

"Don't be silly, I can't sleep in my clothes. They're all I have here." She folded her slacks and sweater neatly and set them aside. Retrieving the quilt, she wrapped it about her sarong-fashion, then lay down beside him. "Share your pillow with me?"

"Bloody hell, you can't sleep next to me."

"Well, I can't sleep with Jason or Lacy. I don't know them nearly as well as I know you."

He sat up. "That's the most cockeyed female logic ever laid on a man."

She sniffed. "I'm not sleeping on the floor."

"You've taken everything wrong, Kaley."

"Probably," she said. "But I'll be right here if you get a notion to change wrong to right." She turned her back to him. "Night."

"Bloody hell!"

FEELING KEENLY the martyr for the first time since he'd been kicked from the lap of the gods, Slater prowled the house with his sleeping bag, looking for a soft floorboard.

Chapter Eight

"Are you moving in or what?" Lacy asked, walking in unannounced while Kaley was dressing.

Kaley absorbed the frontal attack with a smile. "No, we've been quarantined. Didn't you know?"

"Uncle Slater said we can't go to school on Monday."

The sky was a frostbitten gray, the wind furling and banking the house with powdery snow. The old oak was a bare-limbed sentinel shorn of armament. Kaley shivered. The room had gone chilly. She ran her fingers through her hair. It was a tangled mess. And so was Lacy's. "Do you have a hairbrush? We could fix our hair."

"With ribbons?" Lacy blurted.

Kaley glanced around the room. The thongs Slater used were hanging from a nail. "No, but I can make do with these."

"We'll get in trouble."

Kaley cupped the narrow pointy chin in her hand. "Since when have you ever been afraid of a little trouble?"

Lacy shrugged off Kaley's touch, but Kaley could see the girl was pleased with the backhanded compliment. Ten minutes later she was also pleased with the French braid Kaley made for her. She kept running her hand over the smooth plait while Kaley made her own hair presentable. No sound came from elsewhere in the house. "Where's Slater?" she asked.

"In his truck listening to the weather report on the radio. We don't have a television yet."

"I'll just go tell him good morning. Afterward, I'll make breakfast."

As they moved from Slater's bedroom, Kaley noticed the pads on Lacy's socks were filthy. The house, too, needed a good wash. Dust and sawdust clung to every surface. Spiderwebs linked the overhead beams.

Kaley washed her face in icy water from the bathroom tap and squeezed toothpaste onto her finger for an impromptu toothbrush. All of the bathroom fixtures were new and the tub plumbed, though the tub surround was folded and leaned against a wall. A soft green wallpaper would work wonders.

Both Rutledge house and inhabitants needed a woman's care. But there were other matters more pertinent than wallpaper or dirty socks.

Slater lunged to lock the door—too late. Kaley slipped onto the seat beside him. "It's cold out," she said, breathing in the heated air. A country ballad issued from the radio.

Slater gazed at her through bloodshot eyes. Kaley looked fresh and perky and vital. "Won't do you any good to keep harassing me. What you ought to do is go along home. There's a big storm brewing."

"I've weathered storms before. All kinds. Besides, I gave my word to Jessie that I'd stay. You look a little strung out. Didn't you sleep well?"

"I slept like a bear in hibernation."

"You're growing hair like one, too."

He rubbed his chin. "You don't like beards?"

"I adore beards. They make a man look virile and mysterious." She put her arm along the back of the seat. A lock of his hair rested on his shoulder. She twirled it around her finger. "I could braid your hair for you."

"Keep your hands to yourself, missy."

"Kick my shins, Slater."

He glowered at her. "Stop throwing my words back in my face."

"But, they're such fine words, darling. Remember how well they worked on me?" She cocked her head. "I'm still all achy and tingling from last night."

He reached across her and flung open the door, allowing in a blast of icy air. "Get out of my truck."

"You're a bear in the morning, dear heart," she said with silky serenity. "Bet you haven't had your coffee, yet. Breakfast will be ready in about thirty minutes."

"I'm not hungry."

"I am," she said, slamming the door on the double entendre.

Thirty minutes later, almost to the second, Slater pushed through the back door carrying an armload of firewood. Without speaking or looking her way, he passed through to the living room.

But Kaley saw his glance fall briefly upon the table where a steaming bowl of oatmeal topped with brown sugar and milk kept company with a platter of scrambled eggs and a pile of oven toast—all of which she'd prepared on the shiny new stove.

She was unhappy with the coffee because Slater didn't own a proper pot. Still, once the grounds settled, it wasn't half bad. And the aroma was every bit as tempting as the most alluring perfume.

"At least you make oatmeal without lumps," Lacy said. "I hate lumps. They look like snot bubbles."

Kaley put down her spoon. "Thank you."

Jason slid from his chair. "Can we play with our pumpkins again?"

Kaley assured him it was fine with her. They carried their handiwork into the living room, plopping down before the fire Slater had built up.

Some few minutes later he was in the kitchen, ostensibly looking for his misplaced hammer.

"Oatmeal and toast taste a lot better than crow," she said.

He sighed and lowered himself into a chair. "You're relentless, aren't you?"

"When I have to be," she replied, peering at him with an unblinking steadiness.

She poured herself a refill and sat opposite him. He had shaved and slicked back his hair with water. There was a bluish cast in the skin beneath his eyes. "How's your temperature this morning?"

"Steady on," he prevaricated, knowing full well the fever lingered. "If you think you can get to me through kindness, the kids or my stomach, you have another think coming.''

''I'm being pleasant because I like being pleasant. But you chose the weapons. Really, when you consider it, I'm the one on the defensive. I have to use what's available to me, flex my muscles, so to speak.'' She went on conversationally as if discussing weather and not a crucial issue. ''You knock my socks off, Slater. It may come to nothing, but I can't turn my feelings on and off like a faucet. You've already taken up residence in my head.''

The sound of his breath was all chopped up. He was awed by her audacity, or at least as close to being awed as he was ever likely to be. ''We'll agree you've put me on notice.''

''Yes, well, sex aside—and you're not off the hook there—I thought you ought to know how it is with me.'' She smiled sweetly over the rim of her cup. ''That way, when I fight dirty, you won't take it amiss.''

Slater couldn't resist a grin. ''So you think I'm a goner?''

''It's fine with me if you think it necessary to draw this thing out. I understand about men having to save face, especially one with a whopping ego like yours.''

Her cheerful declaration snagged him. He laughed outright. ''That's downright magnanimous of you, missy.''

''I know.'' She took her cup to the sink. ''That huge crate on the back porch, is that the hot-water heater?''

It took Slater a few seconds to shift from battle station to kitchen. ''Yes, why?''

"Could you install it this morning? And perhaps put in the tub surround? I'd love a good soak tonight."

"You can wait until you get home to bathe."

"I can't. My whole body smells of you. It's keeping me in a state of high excitement."

Slater closed his eyes.

Kaley lowered her voice against the children eavesdropping. "What's worse is, even though you're clothed from neck to toe, I can *see* you naked, *feel* every part of you against me."

"I'll put in the tub and water heater."

"I have a kind of horrible airy feeling in my stomach, too. I hope I'm not coming down with whatever you have."

"Make friends with Lacy," he warned stonily. "Because you're not sleeping in my bed tonight."

Kaley accepted with grace that she'd won the skirmish. "Before you start in the bathroom, would you please stoke up this old monstrosity of a wood stove? I can heat water to scrub with and keep the kitchen toasty warm at the same time."

"Scrub what?"

"The kitchen for a start. I like to stay busy. I'm not the kind of person who can just sit around on my duff and daydream all day." She glanced out the snow-rimmed kitchen window. "Won't it be awful if this turns out to be a whopper of a blizzard and Jessie can't get up here tomorrow? We'll have to figure out something to keep the children busy." She took a sip of coffee. "And ourselves, of course." She glanced at him then, her gray eyes wide. "You couldn't have known, but the inside of my elbow is one of my erogenous zones."

"I have to hand it to you, missy. You're entertaining the hell out of me."

She took her cup to the sink so that he wouldn't see her smile. Then, passing behind him, she stood there a moment admiring the width and breadth of his shoulders, the proud way he held his head. She placed her hands on his shoulders.

He tensed, but didn't shake her off. Taking heart, she ran her fingers beneath his hair and up his neck, feeling a warmth some degrees above the norm. She massaged his neck gently.

I know what's wrong with me and it isn't contagious. A spike of fear deflated the airy bubble in her stomach.

"You're not terribly sick, are you, Slater?"

He bolted from the hypnotic effect her hands had on him. "Only in the head, missy. Stop pestering me."

"You're impossible."

She left him to finish his breakfast alone and wandered the house taking mental inventory. Curious, Lacy and Jason tailgated her.

The place had more the look of a camp under siege than a home. Beds were new, but covers consisted of pillows and sleeping bags. Shelves were packed with an array of goods; lightbulbs and nails kept company with unpaired socks, schoolbooks and socket wrenches. Clothes spilled out of suitcases and cardboard boxes. Still, it wasn't any worse than the Jackson homestead had appeared when she'd first laid eyes on it.

Independent passed through her mind. He was probably chewing nails of outrage by now and planning a verbal assault against her being in his enemy's camp overnight. She'd square it with him somehow. But that was later. It was the present she was concerned with.

In an icy room at the foot of the wide hall, she discovered a room filled with cartons as yet unopened.

"What's all of this?" she asked of the children.

"Our things," Lacy said. "They came from our apartment."

"Let's unpack some."

"Uncle Slater won't let us. We don't have anyplace to put it."

Kaley picked up the nearest carton. "We're going to make places," she said. "Let's take some boxes into the living room where it's warm."

Lacy balked. "But when our mother comes, we'll just have to pack stuff up again to take with us."

Jason lifted the top of a box and gasped happily. "Hey! Here're my Legos and dump trucks." He picked up the box and marched past Lacy. She gave him a traitorous glower.

"What we need are towels and linens," Kaley told her. "When your mother comes, I'll help you repack anything you want to take with you." As a secondary inducement she added, "If you locate a couple of cake pans, I could put together a mayonnaise cake for supper."

"Just towels and cake pans?" Lacy repeated, steely-eyed.

"Well, a bowl to mix it in and a wooden spoon."

"That's all?"

"Unless you find something you think would be helpful," Kaley said, and left Lacy to make the decision.

Discovering Slater had left the kitchen, she stood on the threshold, looking at it. The two stoves side by side, one modern and the other ancient lent the kitchen the air of an old lady dressed to the nines with her wig askew and dirt between her toes.

She pushed up her sleeves and went to work. While rearranging the floor-to-ceiling shelves that had once held the harvest of summer fruit and vegetables, but now were home to all manner of beans and Vienna sausage, she came across a canned chicken. She scoured an old iron pot and put the chicken to stew atop the wood-burning stove.

"What's that smell?" Lacy asked, arriving with an armload of linen.

"Manna from heaven. Do you like chicken and dumplings?"

"I like anything except beans." Lacy thawed to the point of a tentative smile. "When I grow up I'm never going to feed my kids beans unless they're in chili. I like chili with beans on hotdogs."

"You're positively gorgeous when you smile, Lacy. You ought to do it more often, and that braid is becoming, too."

Lacy's face flushed. "I'm not supposed to."

Kaley was taken back. "What? Smile?"

"Because my daddy died. It's mourning."

Kaley scooped Lacy up and deposited her on the tabletop. Too surprised to disallow it, Lacy sat there, her thin legs dangling.

"My husband died, too, but he wouldn't like it if I was glum all the time or made those around me unhappy."

"Did he shoot himself?"

Suicide! Kaley swallowed. "No, he died in a truck crash. He went over the side of a mountain."

"Did he do it on purpose?"

"No—but I still felt, well—rejected. I was angry, too. I thought he should've been more careful. You're angry, aren't you?"

Silence.

"A little bit angry?"

"Maybe."

Kaley drew in a ragged breath. A conversation of this sort with a child was virgin territory, but she understood the pain the child harbored. "You speak about your mother a lot. Are you perchance a little bit angry with her, too?"

Lacy's features furled like a closed umbrella. "I guess. Mothers aren't supposed to run away with a man and leave their kids."

"That's true. You must miss her a lot."

"Jason was just a baby. He couldn't even walk, yet." Lacy rolled her eyes. "Or use the bathroom by himself."

"I'll bet you learned how to change his diapers."

Lacy nodded. "It was awful."

"I don't know the first thing about changing diapers. I've never been around babies."

"It's easy. When you get a baby, I'll show you how."

"I'll hold you to that."

There was a frightening element to all this: Slater was providing food and shelter, but other deeper needs were going unmet. When had Lacy last been hugged, Kaley wondered, aching to displace the stoic reserve and shower the taut little package of bones with affection.

"Mom might even come to get us before Christmas. If she gets Aunt Willie's letter soon."

Wary of feeding a hope that might not, most probably wouldn't become reality, Kaley said, "I'd hate to see you leave the mountain. I was really lonesome before you came."

"You mean before Uncle Slater came," Lacy said slyly.

Kaley paused to think that one out. "Well, I had a grown-up lonesome and an ordinary lonesome. You and Jason fill the ordinary lonesome."

"You can get your own kids."

"I'd like to do that one day," Kaley answered, ignoring the returning hostility. "Have you made any friends at school?"

Lacy looked down at her feet and shook her head. "School sucks. I don't need any friends."

"Well, I do," Kaley ventured. "I wish we could be friends."

Lacy heaved a sigh and slipped from the table.

Kaley plucked at the stack of linen, found sheets, dishcloths and pillow slips. "Hey! These are terrific."

Lacy shied her eyes away from Kaley. "I'll think about being your friend. But don't cook any beans."

Kaley made a face of mock horror. "I wouldn't dare."

Later, when Slater came through the kitchen on his way to the back porch, Kaley waylaid him. "Take a coffee break?"

"No."

"I had a talk with Lacy earlier. She said her dad killed himself." A curtain fell over his features.

"So?"

"I just wanted you to know I understand now why you feel so committed, so unwilling to take on any more emotional baggage."

This was skittish territory. He arched a brow. "What's your point, missy?"

"I think you're wonderfully unselfish to dedicate yourself to those kids."

"Swell."

"It has to be daunting and scary to be responsible for others, especially when you're not used to it."

"Is that it?"

"No. I'm going to help you."

"How will I bear up under all this magnanimity?"

"Men!" Kaley said, resigned. "You all bury emotions beneath sarcasm and snide remarks."

"I beg your pardon."

Her eyes took on a smoky look. "Granted—this time. Lacy is confused. She feels rejected. I know that feeling. It's terrible."

"Okay, missy. I'm a worm."

"I wasn't talking about last night, smarty. That, I've filed in the realm of you showing off your admirable fortitude. I'm talking about a whole lifetime of not seeming able to do the right thing. Never having approval from my parents. I'm talking about Virgil dying and leaving me alone. And Independent is always thinking up ruses to get me off the mountain."

"That's no wonder. You're meddlesome. Won't leave a man in peace."

She tossed her head. "It's nice to know that if the two of you get over the hump of a thirty-year-old grievance, you'll have a lot in common. I'm going to take Lacy and Jason under my wing as much as they'll allow me to. If you give permission, they can stop by after school. I could help them with homework, take them to the movies—"

He snorted. "A glorified Girl Scout."

She smiled winningly. "As it happens, in my youth, I was an ace of a Girl Scout. What do you say? Any objections?"

"I can think of a hundred, but you'll probably lie in wait and lure them to your cottage like the wicked witch in Hansel and Gretel."

"I only feel wicked around you. I've been thinking about that, too."

"I have a hot-water heater to install," he said.

"I admit I have a crush on you," she said hurriedly. Slater turned back. "But I see now that's all it is." She flicked her hand dismissively. "An adolescent thing, really. You're the first man to come along after Virgil. My hormones went awry. I was so *intense.* And fogged with fever, well, you weren't thinking straight, either. I guess that's why you thought we were falling in love.'' She sighed like a dulcimer plucked off-key. ''I'm mortified that I let you undress me, see me naked—''

''Bull Durham!'' Slater exclaimed in outraged admiration. ''Excellent performance, missy, but I don't buy it.''

Kaley wrinkled her nose. ''Shoot. Where'd I go wrong?''

''You dumb hussy,'' he said softly, ready to take her into his arms and prove her reasoning faulty. ''You *gloried* in being naked. You aren't crediting my memory.''

Oh, yes I am. She shrugged. ''Oh, well, if you need any help with the hot-water heater, let me know.'' With an inward smile she turned back to rearranging the shelves. *Hussy. Heavens! The conceit of the man.*

Slater stepped outside. The frigid air seared his lungs, but felt refreshing on his face and neck, which blazed heatedly. The back of his neck throbbed with the intermittent tattoo of a drum corps. It was bearable. So that was all right.

What wasn't all right was Kaley. He was captivated. He could resist thrusting breast and cocked hip from now to Hades, but her outlandish theater had a currency difficult to ignore. Especially now that his defenses were cracked.

He laughed aloud. Cracked? Bloody hell. His defenses were down around his ankles like his pants were last night. If his gonads were anything to judge by, they had sure put ''paid'' to that old adage that you didn't miss what you never had.

He missed all right. Kaley was reaching her tendrils right inside him.

He could tell her.

Listen, missy, I've got this thing growing deep inside my brain. It's benign, but inoperable. No, that's not true. The bloody surgeons are willing to use the knife, but there's a fifty-fifty chance I'd end up an imbecile or blind or paralyzed right there in the cutting room.

Now, I'm still gonna end up like that, only it's gonna take longer, say three to five years, provided the damned thing doesn't have a growth spurt and whack me out overnight.

All that teasing glee and warm incandescence lighting her gray eyes like warm smoke would evaporate. Not entirely perhaps, but it'd be joined by pity. And hope.

And the worse he got, more pity and less hope.

If he had any sense, and he counted himself a man with an inordinate amount of that trait, he'd throw himself and the kids into the truck and get the hell off the mountain until Aunt Willie could take over the kids. Then he'd find himself a hidey-hole out in a desert somewhere until he was ready for buzzards to pick his bones. A good clean ending. Not like the cop-out stunt Jerome had pulled.

On the other hand, lying that low held no appeal. It smacked of tainting his integrity.

But staying meant he was headed hell-for-leather into perilous territory with Kaley Jackson.

He inhaled. The cold air jolted. His gaze fell on the hot-water heater. It had a guaranteed life of five years.

Bloody hell! The machine would live a longer, more useful life than he would.

Having put it precisely into thought for the first time, Slater felt a small twinge of fear at the prospect of his future, and this struck him as abysmal.

"Good crying damn!" he muttered and wedged an unlighted cigar between his teeth.

He demolished the packing crate with his hands.

UNOBSERVED and with some circumspection, Kaley was watching Slater through the window that faced the back porch.

For long minutes he was preoccupied with thought, his unblinking gaze disdaining the wind that spit snow into his eyes.

When his glance shifted to stare at the crated heater, his expression was implacable as steel, and she sensed he'd made some irrevocable decision.

She stifled an awed gasp as he suddenly began to yank apart the crate with his bare hands in a cataclysm of raw violence. Once the shiny white water heater was revealed amid the splintered wood, he stepped back, dug in his pocket for matches, cupped his hand against the wind and lighted his cigar. He inhaled deeply and contemplated the heater with immense satisfaction.

Whatever his thoughts—and she was ready to offer a pound of pennies for their revelation—she knew they'd been abandoned with the wreckage strewn along the porch and out into the snow.

Caught up in her own introspection, he had to bang on the door with his boot before she realized he'd hoisted the heater to his shoulder and wanted her to let him in.

"Give me a hand," he said with no trace of the spent violence she'd witnessed. "Guide the tail of this thing so it doesn't bang into any walls."

"You must've bought the biggest hot-water heater in Fentress County," she observed, putting her hands on it and following him through the house.

"I use a lot of water."

She smiled. "I can imagine."

At the entrance to the bathroom, he wrested the tank off his back. She stood on the threshold. "Can I help in any way?"

"No thanks. I've got the nook all prepped. No need for you to stand around offering caustic comments."

"You do good work with your hands, Slater." She moved past him into the bathroom, carelessly allowing her hand to trail across his shoulders as she went. She sat on the rim of the tub. "Actually, you have wonderful hands. I've been noticing."

"Get out of here. You're a worse pest than the kids."

"Okay. I'm going." She didn't budge, instead, walked her fingertips along the rim of the tub. "Have you ever done it in the tub?"

He muttered an oath, picked her up by her waist and put her outside the room. Holding her at bay, he said: "In the tub, in the shower, in a hay rick, in the swamp and in the desert. Does that satisfy your interest?"

Her eyes twinkled with an elemental insouciance. "Absolutely. I'm impressed. Would you consider an invitation to tea caustic? My pumpkin pie is in the stove warmer, defrosting. About twenty minutes?''

''I suppose if I refuse, you'll think up something else to distract me.''

''Since I'm exceptionally resourceful—yes.''

He uttered a pained sigh. ''Tea wouldn't go amiss.''

Chapter Nine

"Breakfast, high tea, and now cake after dinner," Slater said, forking the last morsel of mayonnaise cake into his mouth. "You're spoiling us, missy."

"It's all right with me if you get used to it." She began to clear the table, putting the dishes in the sink to soak.

He shook his head, dislodging a grin. "Give it up, love."

"Won't."

"I could eat dumplings every day," Jason piped enthusiastically. "They're my favorite now."

Kaley kissed the top of his head. "Thank you. Applause is always welcome. Would coffee and brandy go down well in front of the fireplace?" she asked Slater.

"I ought to refuse."

She smiled enticingly. "The brandy is my Halloween treat, remember? If you don't accept, I'll have to think up a trick."

"I'm a beaten man," he said, and contradicted that by laughing.

"Listen," Lacy said, cocking her head. "The wind's stopped."

Kaley glanced out the window. "So has the snow." She wrinkled her nose in disappointment. "Those few inches on the ground won't stop Jessie. You're a lucky man, Slater Rutledge."

"God knows better," he joked, though he acknowledged mentally that while in Kaley's company he had for hours on end disregarded the consistent throb in his head, the sometime ache in his limbs.

For weeks past almost everything he'd done or thought had been dominated by the medical pronouncement dumped in his lap. There was no question that Kaley was cheerfully leading him into tricky areas, emotionally and physically. Perhaps it was his common sense that was being affected above all. Because if he had any sense left, he'd come out from behind his barricade of logic and allow her to reel him in on her invisible line.

The kids were all for bundling up and going outside to build a snowman in the waning light. Lacy was insistent. "We never had this much snow in Atlanta."

Kaley appealed to Slater. "Let's do."

On the premise that if one adult agreed, permission had been granted, the children raced to find their jackets.

Slater rose from the table. "I suppose playing in the snow is safer than sitting in front of a cozy fire with a determined nymph."

Kaley smiled over at him and fluttered her lashes shamelessly. "I like the nymph part."

"I'll just get my hat and coat," he said.

As they filed out the back door, Kaley whispered to him. "Nymphs know how to do more than cook and clean and play in the snow."

He gauged the depth of her eyes, then studied her mouth. Her smile had no subtext at all. The swift current of desire that swam through him approximated something like torture. "I'm aware of all your other skills, missy."

The snow was too dry and powdery for building anything, but Lacy and Jason found immense satisfaction in frolicking in it, scooping up great handfuls and throwing it up into the air and running beneath it.

The winds had carried away the last gray cloud, leaving the air sharply crisp. "We'll have a moon and stars tonight," Kaley observed, then lowering her eyes from the heavens, she pointed to fencing that jutted away from the old barn. "You're serious about horses. That's a new corral."

He lighted up a cigar and inhaled. "I like horses. They'd be a start."

"Then what?"

"Then we'll see."

Kaley looked at him, his face was closed, his mouth a thin line gripping the cigar. She wondered if she would ever possess a knowledge of his interior self, his private aspects that failed to show on the surface. An idea brushed past her as briefly as though a bird had flown past her from a low bush. "You're not certain you're going to stay on the mountain, are you?"

"I'm not certain of anything in this life, missy."

The tone of his voice daunted her. Feeling all at once the weight of her skittering fears about him, she sat on a low stump. "I am. I'm certain I'm never going to leave these hills. It felt like coming home when Virgil brought me here. It's not paradise..." She cocked her head. "Or maybe it is. Mine, anyway.

"Early on when I began gathering grapevines, I came upon a doe with a deformed leg. It's shorter than her others and kind of drags. She had a fawn with her. I've only seen her one other time since, but I can tell her hoof marks in mud or snow. Every year I look for her sign to see if she's had a fawn. I feel renewed when I find it. If she can make it, I can, too.

"And every spring I put scraps of yarn on my bedroom windowsill and a pair of redbirds use it to line their nest. A black snake lives under my front porch. He's a real gentleman, too. He never suns himself on the steps, but takes himself off to the graveyard and stretches out on one of the tombstones. And there's an old grandfather of a possum that hibernates in the barn every winter. He's gotten so old, even Independent has sympathy for him, and tosses a bit of corn his way." She looked toward a distant mountain peak. "I think we have a kind of continuity here not found anywhere else on earth. I like to think that when I'm dead and gone, someone will be putting out scraps of yarn for the next generation of redbirds." She sighed wistfully. "Of course, it'd help if I was producing a next generation myself."

Slater flicked the ashes from his cigar. "Of redbirds?"

She wet her lips and turned to look at him. "Don't act the dunce. You know what I mean."

He was afraid he did, and for a moment he felt terribly sad. She was a woman with passion and humor, a woman with unsuspected sensitivity, a woman a man would never lose his desire for; a woman a man could grow old with—provided the man didn't have a death sentence hanging over his head. "I suppose you want a houseful of the little heathens."

"Don't you?"

"I have two," he said, their chattering and squealing penetrating his interior thoughts. "They're driving me around the bend."

"Once they have routines, they'll settle down. Lacy doesn't have it in her mind yet that this is her home, and that influences Jason."

"They do have regular routines," Slater countered.

"They need a mother."

The chill air was giving a radiance to her cheeks. Slater looked away. "Aunt Willie will fill that slot."

"Oh." Kaley looked down at her loafer-encased feet. Was that it, then?

Her teeth chattered.

"Go on in the house," he advised. "No sense both of us coming down with pneumonia just because those two rotters want to play dive and splat in forty-degree weather."

"I think I will." Her smile was uncertain. "I dressed with the notion of engaging your interest, you know, not the weather. My feet are freezing."

"Kaley."

She turned back. "What?"

"Never mind."

She stared at him steadily for a moment, and the expression of longing in his face chased away her doubts and rendered her strong again. "Slater, as long as it takes, I can wait. You want me as much as I want you. A woman knows these things."

He watched her into the house, wishing he could spit out the harsh words to stop this charade. But truth to tell, he was enjoying it. Perhaps he ought to have her once, if only to confront the true condition of his feelings.

He rewound his thoughts for review and laughed aloud.

So much for practical considerations.

Kaley stood at the kitchen window, watching. His sudden burst of laughter brought the children to his side. They coaxed him into the barn and, after a moment, came out with a piece of cardboard made into an impromptu sled.

Her chest felt suddenly tight. *I want to live this way the rest of my life,* she thought, and turned to start the coffee, measuring out the grounds into cold water.

She grinned. *No, I don't. I absolutely must have a proper coffeepot.*

"RISE AND SHINE, missy. Sun's up."

Kaley glanced sleepy-eyed toward the window. The sun was a prodigious yellow disk rising above an easterly ridge. Lacy's and Jason's pajamas were heaped in a pile on the opposite bed. Disappointment that he had not collected her in the dead of night and taken her off to his bed brought her fully awake.

"You can toot along home. I'm not contagious."

"What?" She bolted upright. "Jessie's here already?"

"Here and gone. It's after ten," Slater said.

"But she promised not to come until after noon!" Kaley wailed.

"She hurried the lab techs."

Kaley threw off the quilts. "I'll fix breakfast first." Her sleeping attire was one of his flannel shirts, which left a lot of leg exposed.

Slater paused to enjoy the view for only a moment before passing a steaming mug under her nose. "Compliments of the house."

Kaley accepted the coffee. "Why'd you let me sleep in?"

"Kept expecting you to wake up. The kids were like banshees. I fed and watered them and sent 'em to play in the barn."

She sipped the coffee. He boiled it as thick as he brewed tea. "What did Jessie say?"

"Just what I told you. I'm not contagious and we're off quarantine."

"But what caused the fever?"

"Ordinary American bacteria, I suspect."

"She said more than that. I know she did." She gazed at him a moment before directing her eyes to the window again, resigned that she now had no obvious reason to linger.

"She said she would talk to you later in the week and that Miss Broom would not be around to give the kids their homework assignments seeing as they're only missing one day and can make it up in class."

"Slater, you're frustrating me. If you don't tell me what she said about *you* I'm going to stand up and yank this shirt off and race around the house naked."

"I have a slight infection for which I'm to stop in and see a particular doctor who will give me a prescription for an antibiotic. That ease you?"

"Yes. As long as you have every intention of seeing that particular doctor."

"When time permits. At the moment I'm fit as a fiddle."

A fire stirred in her belly. "The children are in the barn, you say?"

He allowed himself another brief look at her, then shook his head. "You have to go home, Kaley. Now."

The urgency in his voice alerted her. "Are you having second thoughts about us?"

A faint trace of scarlet seared his cheekbones. "Lots of thoughts and reasons why not."

She sighed. "I wish I had the courage, or better yet, the lack of integrity to beg."

Slater jammed his hands in his pockets to keep himself from taking her into his arms. "I have work to do, missy. Get dressed."

"All right." She handed him the coffee mug with a glance calculated to inflame. "Want to watch?"

"You crazy little pervert," he said throatily, masking the hunger in his eyes. "I ought to take you up on that just to teach you some manners."

He turned and strode out of the room.

On the porch when she was taking her leave of him, she held out her hand. "Friends?"

He accepted her hand, holding it a moment before releasing it. "Friends. That is, as long as you don't come bearing gifts of pumpkin brandy."

"I'm sorry about that. Independent said it was his best. Does your throat still feel scorched?"

"Did it occur to you that the old man, suspecting it was for me, might have added a dollop of something or other?"

"He wouldn't."

"Then save it in case you ever come upon a dragon with clogged pipes."

"Tell the children goodbye for me?"

"Will do."

He watched her drive off. The back tires of the truck slewed dangerously on the narrow snow-slick lane. His heart leaped to his throat, but she corrected and without looking back, threw out her hand and gave him a jaunty wave.

Abruptly he sat on the steps, leaned his elbows on his knees and wondered how life had suddenly become so complicated.

He thought of the tender curve of Kaley's bottom lip, the teasing mischief in her eyes. Falling in love was not part of the master plan. The last thing he intended was to find himself—on top of all else—with heart problems.

Sex had always been a lark; fun, impulsive, satisfying, as far as it went. The deep abyss of emotional bondage had not been engaged. But good crying damn, it was engaged now.

The expression on her face as she had kneeled naked on his bed was etched indelibly into his brain.

He wondered if she guessed it had cost him a piece of his soul to put her away from him.

Lacy and Jason came racing around the house and stopped short, glancing from him to the tire tracks in the snow.

"Kaley's gone?" Jason said, openly dismayed.

"She had to get along home. You're to stop in her place after school tomorrow, if you want."

Eyeing him with her single-minded scrutiny, Lacy rocked on her heels. "Kaley likes you."

Slater recognized the bland measure of cynicism in the statement. And why shouldn't he? Both he and Lacy had been subjected to the sharp end of Jerome's fierce self-rightousness. Pity the child's mother had not hung around to soften it for her. "Yes, she does," he told her, and left it at that. "C'mon into the house. I'll make us a cup of tea. It'll warm us up."

Lacy wrinkled her nose. "You make god-awful tea, Slater."

"What's this Slater business, missy?" he asked, challenging her as they entered the welcoming warmth of the house.

"That's what Kaley calls you. It's your name."

"That selfsame Kaley thinks I brew a terrific cup of tea."

"That's what she *says.* When you're not looking, she pours it down the sink."

"You just love to tattle, don't you?"

"Only on grown-ups," she said flippantly, her usual solemn face breaking into a grin and giving him a glimpse of the whimsical child beneath the gruff and scruffy exterior.

He felt a tug on his heartstrings. The experience of taking care of the children was affecting him more than he would've guessed.

Bloody hell! Before the day was done, he was going to pen a note to Aunt Willie and insist she get her crotchety old arse up here before he went completely wacko.

KALEY THOUGHT she'd met the dragon when she entered her house. Independent was breathing fire.

"Stop puffing up like the most pleased old boy in Fentress County and tell me the meaning of this," she insisted, kicking aside the piles of clothing that lay scattered about the living room floor.

He smirked. "Just helping you pack. Figured since you took up permanent-like with a Rutledge—"

"We were quarantined by Jessie. She left you a note, telling you."

"Note, smote. Sleep with him, did you?"

"If I had, it wouldn't be any of your business." She gasped. "Did you do any damage to my drying sheds?"

"Naw. Didn't have time. Flossie's feeling poorly. Had to tend to her."

Kaley started to scoop up an armload of her clothes, stopped and straightened. "Did you put something in that brandy?"

"Course not," he said, offended.

"Slater said it didn't taste right."

"What did you expect for a dime? Perfection? Anyways, the Rutledges ain't used to nothin' but raw liquor." He cackled happily. "Set the feller on fire, did it?"

"I'm out of patience with you, Independent. Another thing. You might as well know I'm taking those kids under my wing, so they'll be stopping by often. I expect you to be civil about it."

He snorted. "You ain't got the makin's for motherin'."

That stung. "Yes, I do," she shot back, a thread of clarity dawning. The insouciant lever she'd used on Slater might as easily work on Independent. "You're just jealous."

"Piffle! Of what?"

"Oh, that I'm paying attention to someone else." She eyed the clothes at his feet. "At least it's nice to know you missed me."

"Huh? I ain't said no such thing."

"Actions speak louder than words."

"Growin' up a flatlander warped your mind."

"Drinking your own rotgut has warped yours."

"The least Virgil coulda done afore he died was teach you to respect your elders."

"Virgil taught me more than that, you vile old thing. He taught me to love you."

Independent's eyes disappeared into the baggy folds of skin that draped his face. "You drunk on some of that pumpkin brandy?"

Kaley spied plaid among the helter-skelter on the floor. "Hey! That's my old wool poncho." She retrieved it and shook it out. "I can make this over for Lacy."

Independent uttered a noise deep in his throat. "I ain't got time for foolishness. I got to see to Flossie."

Kaley became serious. The mule was more a pet than a work animal. Independent "talked over" things with Flossie. He lavished affection on her and fed her special tidbits of sugar cubes and apples. When her teeth were hurting, he boiled corn and pumpkins into mash and fed her by hand.

"Have you called in a vet?"

He gave a hoot of disgust.

"Slater knows about horses. Mules can't be that different. Maybe he can help."

"I ain't havin' a Rutledge layin' hands on anything I own," he said bitterly. "Thelma Broom is comin'. She knows potions."

"Well, you know best. Suit yourself."

He sniffed. "Aim to."

When Kaley returned from town, where she shipped orders and stopped by Wal-Mart to buy some games for Lacy and Jason, Thelma Broom's ancient car was parked up near the barn.

It was as good a time as any to look in on Flossie. Independent was bound to be more hospitable in Miss Broom's presence.

The old building was a testimony to generations of Jacksons, and an antique collector's dream.

The walls were hung with handmade saddles, old ropes, spinning wheels, hand plows, wood-shaping awls and the necessary tools of a life lived a hundred years or more ago. Handmade tongue-and-groove boxes and trunks held everything from an old-fashioned meat grinder to candle molds and iron pots used to boil down the fats of animals and the saps of trees. The barn was Independent's territory, and Kaley was seldom allowed to browse.

The air was redolent with the smell of Flossie, dust and baled hay. Kaley could hear Independent cooing to the old mule.

She leaned over the stall gate. Miss Broom looked up from Flossie's flanks. Holding a pail aloft, she said, "Comfrey—good for what ails a mule and terrific for complexions."

Kaley laughed. "If that's your secret, I'll take a jar."

At the sound of her voice, Flossie snorted and her ears swept back.

"Outta here," Independent growled. "You're upsetting my mule."

"I just wanted to let you know I was home." She turned to go.

"Wait up," Miss Broom called. "I'll walk up to the house with you."

While Kaley poured soft drinks, Miss Broom went through the house to the bathroom to rid herself of "the smell of mule." She returned to the kitchen wearing curiosity like an old shawl. "Are all those clothes turned out on your floor destined for the rag bin or a lap rug?"

"Neither. That's Independent's devilment at work. I left them there on purpose. I'm going to sort through them for possibles to make up some clothes for Lacy Rutledge."

"What in the world provoked that old dinosaur to paw through your things?"

Kaley hesitated. "I thought you knew. I spent a couple of days at Slater's. Jessie quarantined us because Slater had a fever and she thought it might be some exotic disease and contagious. Independent didn't approve of my being there."

Miss Broom didn't blink. "Well, I approve, my dear, but you look soul-tired. Is something bothering you?"

Kaley drew circles on the table with her glass. She wasn't about to discuss the intimacy she and Slater had shared, or it's shortfall, but she wasn't ashamed of loving him. "I just wish Independent would be more understanding, or at least, not so spiteful."

Miss Broom chortled softly. "Honey, have you ever wondered why preachers rail so against hate and revenge?"

"Well—they're sins."

Miss Broom laughed. "You dear innocent. There's sin and then there's sin. Hate and revenge are so satisfyingly *filling*. That's what you're up against with Independent. He's occupying all of himself with the only thing left to him—spite, bitterness, anger. Even old goats like him are romantics, or were once. They think themselves and all they own are immortal. They can't cope when reality strikes. Some men take to drink, some to gambling, some, like Independent, take to bitterness. The taste of it is so wonderfully tart. Keeps him on his toes."

"I'd laugh, but you're almost making sense."

"Of course I'm making sense. Independent isn't going to get shut of that satisfying feeling unless he's got something to replace it. Tell you this much, I wouldn't want to be living up here when that old mule dies.''

Alarm swam through Kaley. ''*Is* Flossie dying?''

Miss Broom nodded. ''I doubt the old swayback will survive to year's end. She's got croup, brittle bones and she's blind.'' She sighed. ''It happens to the best of us.''

''Oh, Lord.''

''And don't expect him to have the vet put her down. He's got the notion that a vet's an agent for the glue factory, and some of them are.'' She reached across the table and patted Kaley's hand. ''Don't look so glum. Think about buying the old dinosaur something live for Christmas.''

Suddenly all Kaley's circuits were on overload. Her business was going down the tubes, her parents' disinheriting her, Slater rejecting her, Independent's spite. She'd never been a superwoman. What made her think she could keep up the farce?

She burst into tears.

Miss Broom came around and squeezed her shoulders. ''There now. Everything will work out for the best. You'll see.''

''It didn't for Independent,'' she said, hiccuping.

''Of course it has. He's just too stubborn to see it. In spite of all his troubles, he's living his life exactly as it suits him.''

Kaley licked the salty taste of tears from her lips. Miss Broom handed her a napkin and she blew her nose. ''I'm sorry I broke down like that.''

''Pooh. Tears undo the soiling of our souls. It won't stretch me to do two good deeds in one day,'' she went on. "I'm inviting myself to supper and cooking it. You go along and take a toasty soak in the tub with some of those lovely bath salts you keep on the shelf in there."

"That's not a half-bad idea," she agreed. Warm baths had the effect of hemming all her frayed emotions. In the weeks following Virgil's death she had bathed two or three times a day, as if the hysteria and numbness within her overflowed and needed the outlet of bathwater to drain away.

Yet, as she soaped herself, Kaley felt as though she was washing away the magic of the weekend with Slater. The ache in her loins was suddenly so overwhelmingly stimulating, she gasped.

I'm obsessed, she thought dispassionately, and that clarity gave way to an image of her mother.

Perhaps obsessiveness was genetic. Her mother had obsessed on her. Miram Sloan had continued pursuing a career in languages after Kaley was born. Now that Kaley thought about it, Miram had spent an inordinate amount of time focusing on her daughter. Had Miram surrendered herself to what she saw as her role of "mother" in an attempt to fulfill an unidentified emptiness? If so, Kaley had fallen woefully short of fulfilling her mother's needs.

If Miss Broom was right about Independent filling himself with bitterness, could it be that her mother had filled herself with criticism? To whom the bitterness or the criticism was directed didn't matter one whit. What mattered was how it felt to its progenitor.

It was a new way of looking at her relationship with her mother.

Kaley felt all at once lighter, freed in good measure from the burden of hurt the years of criticism had endowed.

She went to the kitchen table wrapped in her terry robe and her hair only towel-dried.

"I took Independent a plate," Miss Broom said. "He's not about to be coaxed away from Flossie for more than a minute or two."

"I'm going to invite my folks up for Christmas," Kaley said.

Miss Broom's fork was in the shadow of her mouth. Sensing Kaley's statement was something momentous, she put it down. "They've never been here, have they?"

"I've deliberately kept them distant. Growing up, I was a trophy to be trotted out for the world. Their world anyway. I've always known that nothing I did was ever good enough or right or proper—until now."

"What changed your mind?"

"What you said about emptiness."

Miss Broom looked thoughtful. "Having them here might not change any of that," she said gently.

"I know. But I've changed. I've often thought I needed their approval to be a success. I wanted their approval so badly it colored everything I did. I figured it out. Independent fills up his emptiness with anger and spite, like you said. The parallel is that my mother filled herself with criticism. I'm just the catchall for it. It's no reflection on me. It's her."

Miss Broom forked up the meat loaf and chewed thoughtfully. "You're going to be a wise old woman one day."

Kaley smiled at the older woman, noticing for the first time that Miss Broom had extraordinary violet eyes, deep and caring and somehow sad. "Miss Broom, have you ever been in love?"

"Why—why, yes, actually."

"You didn't marry him?"

Her eyes glistened. "World War Two got in the way."

"Is his name on the war memorial in the courthouse yard?"

"Yes, you nosy young thing. Now, eat that meat loaf before it congeals on your plate." Her eyes twinkled. "And, you, my dear, are you in love?"

Kaley grinned. "Why—why yes, actually."

"Is his name engraved on the war memorial in the courthouse yard?"

Kaley glowed. "No, but we're on battle stations."

They broke into giggles like ten-year-olds.

Independent burst into the kitchen. "What's so funny?"

Miss Broom caught her breath. "Old men like you."

"Here's your durn plate," he said, plopping it on the table, then he made an about-face and exited the kitchen in a huff.

Kaley sobered. "Something alive? You mean like another mule?"

"Or a puppy, a kitten, baby chicks, a piglet. Anything that needs nurturing so that he has to go outside himself to look after it."

Kaley propped her elbows on the table and rested her chin in her hands. "When I first came here, I should've let him know how helpless I felt instead of brazening it out.''

''Awfully hard to do, seeing as he had a broken hip and you had to help him put on his drawers.''

Kaley sighed. ''Why do men make such a big deal about what's between their legs?''

Miss Broom laughed. ''My dear, because *we* do.''

Thinking of Slater, Kaley blushed.

Chapter Ten

Slater heard the clanging of the cowbell, but it was the thundering of the hooves that came up through the ground beneath his boots that got his attention. For a moment he was transported back to Australia and bouncing in the saddle as he raced over hillock and down gullies herding wild and canny broomies.

Then the shouting reached his ears and he recognized Kaley's voice. He placed the ax in the truck bed and leaned against the tailgate, booted feet crossed, waiting for adventure to come to him on the narrow lane that zigzagged up the mountain.

The old mule came hell-bent around a sharp bend, teeth bared, gray haunches dripping lather.

Slater swept his hat off his head and windmilled his arms. ''Hiii! Yiii!''

The mule stopped in her tracks.

''Whoa, girl,'' he crooned softly, taking a step toward her, then another. The animal's chest heaved, but her eyes watched and her ears twitched at his every step. ''Easy, old girl…'' he murmured, keeping his hat at the side of his leg, ready to swing it out should the mule decide to bolt. Her ears flattened when he was within grabbing distance of her halter. His voice became softer.

"Good girl...you've had yourself a high old time...hold still." He whistled tunelessly under his breath. His hand came up slowly and he patted her neck, rubbing the top of her foreleg then moving his hand up to curl his fingers around her halter.

Kaley rounded the bend in the road. "Catch her!" she yelled at Slater the same instant Independent burst out of the forest on his right.

"Hey! Git your hands off my mule!"

"Before you've got her in hand or after, old man?"

"Now! You cussed weasel-looking varmint!" he yelled between heaving breaths. His chest was pumping fitfully, his face flushed, his gnarled old hands trembling from exertion.

"Don't bust a gut," Slater said, worried that the old swagman would have a stroke. He took his hand away from Flossie and stepped back. The mule did a dance, kicked and took off at a trot back down the lane.

"Now, look what you done!" Independent screamed, thrusting out his arms and leaping at Slater. He caught the old man's wrists and held them down. "Ain't you got no respect for your elders? Damn your hide! Turn me loose!"

Kaley grabbed Independent by the back of his shirt. "Stop it!" she cried breathlessly. "Both of you!"

Slater loosened his grip on Independent and stepped back. Kaley stepped between them. "Can't either one of you act civilized?"

Slater leaped at her gall. "Hold on. I was minding my own business, cutting saplings for a fence."

"A Rutledge ain't got no call to go fencing this mountain! I shoulda filled your backside full of buckshot when I had the chance."

Kaley grabbed Independent's arm. "Come on. Flossie's back to the barn by now."

He yanked his arm free. "Git away from me and suck up to him." He spit at Slater's feet. "That's what I think of a Rutledge."

"Get out of here, old man before I forget that you're twice my age."

"Twice and then some, you good-fer-nothin'." He spun around and hiked off down the dirt road, muttering to himself.

Kaley faced Slater and shrugged her shoulders. "I'm sorry. He's been in a foul mood all day. He was trying to get a tonic down Flossie when she bolted."

"No harm done."

"Sure?" She gave him a sideways glance as she brushed her hair back from her face. The sleeves were cut from his denim jacket, and she wondered if he cut the sleeves from much of his wardrobe just to accommodate his power-filled arms—or to show off his tattoos. "That winded me," she said, blaming the lagging catch in her breath on her run up the mountain after Flossie. "I must be out of shape."

"Not from where I'm standing. Your shape looks stupendous."

Her body tensed. "How nice of you to notice."

He laughed, his eyes dark and turbulent. "Some of the old man must've rubbed off. You're all spice today."

"How've you been feeling?"

He gave her a hard look. "Terrific. You?"

"Terrific."

He saw more questions arising in her wide dark eyes. A craving for her began to send darts of desire racing through him. "I was just getting ready to take this load of saplings to the barn. Want to ride with me?"

She had to bite her tongue to keep from throwing caution to the winds and saying yes. "I can't. I'm packing vines to be shipped out today."

He moved around to the driver's side of his truck. "Another time, then. Don't be a stranger."

"I don't count myself a stranger with you, Slater. Not since the night you first kissed me."

He eyed her sharply. "Was that a poisoned dart?"

"No," she said lightly, lifting her chin. "Just a fact."

"Would you like me to toss you in the truck, take you up to the house and put you in my bed?"

"That sounds like a lovely way to spend the afternoon."

"Okay. You talked me into it. Get in."

"Can't, I have work to do."

Before she reached the bend in the road, he called out, "It *was* a poisoned dart."

She didn't look back, but she raised her hand, signing, "Two."

"Damn!" he muttered. But he felt a strange sense of happiness that implied he had a future just waiting to surprise him with all kinds of delights.

He exhaled heavily. Damn!

"HOW LONG are you going to mope around like this?" Jessie eyed Kaley's untouched french fries. "Are you going to eat those?"

Kaley pushed the carton toward her. "I don't know. The rest of my life probably."

Jessie rolled her eyes. "You see him, don't you?"

"Of course. Either at the mailbox or when I walk Lacy and Jason home." And if their hands accidently touched, they burned with excitement; if their eyes met, the hunger was naked, expressing a known quality. Each time she thought he might be caving, he reined in his emotions and shut her out. "I understand what he says about commitment, but I could help."

"You are helping. Miss Broom says the kids are positively blooming. Lacy isn't nearly as rebellious, and her grades are way up."

"Well then, what's my reward?"

"Heaven?"

Kaley clasped her hands together, feeling the dampness in her palms. "There's something terribly wrong with Slater, isn't there?"

Jessie frowned. "Kaley, he knows what I know. What the lab techs said. If he told you—fine. If not, you know I can't discuss clients."

"You do all the time. Measles, mumps, who's pregnant—"

"Common-knowledge items."

"So there *is* something awful with Slater. You're both keeping it from me."

"Stop fishing, and stop looking as if you're about to cry. Listen, he doesn't have any socially unacceptable diseases, if that's what's worrying you. And I shouldn't even be revealing that."

"He told me that. I believe him."

"Well, good."

"So, what is it?"

"Dammit, Kaley, I'm a county nurse, not an internist."

"What do you *suspect?*"

Jessie sighed wearily. "From the blood workup, a simple ordinary inflammation or infection of some sort. Antibiotics should clear it right up."

"His headache never really goes away."

"I can see why not! You're giving me one. Whatever gave you the idea headaches are the exclusive province of women? Give me a break."

Kaley bristled. "You don't have to get so hostile. I only want to know because I care."

"I know."

"Sometimes Slater looks so tired it scares me."

"He is tired. He's retrofitting a dilapidated farm and being nursemaid to two kids. I have single parents in my caseload up against the same thing as Slater. They're aging before my eyes."

"Why did he get an infection in the first place?"

"Good grief—maybe he stuck a nail in his foot, hit his shin with the ax, maybe his immune system is short-circuiting. That happens to the best of us after a death in the family. His brother died, remember?"

Kaley stared off into space. "It's something more. I know it is."

"You're thinking that because he doesn't want to have a heavy relationship with you right now. Stop making it a big deal and respect the man for it. Let's talk about the other man in your life. How's Independent doing?"

Kaley put her frustration with Slater on hold. "On the days Flossie is frisky and he can take her for a trot, he's his ornery old self. When Flossie's down, he's morose. I just hope that mule hangs on until after Christmas. I don't need Independent going splat on me while my folks are here."

"They accepted!"

"Mother called yesterday, asking what kinds of clothes to bring and wanting to know if her sequined cocktail dress would be appropriate."

Jessie hooted. "Oh, boy."

"I suggested long underwear and jeans. She said, 'What a novel idea.'" Her voice quavered. "I hope I know what I'm doing by having them up. When I'm just thinking about Mother, I feel strong, but I dread the first time she says, 'What an awful hairstyle, dear, perhaps you ought to have it shaped, find a style more flattering.'"

"Don't worry about it. Just be yourself."

"That's never worked before."

Jessie gathered her pursc and briefcase. "I've got to hit the road. I'm teaching a parenting class tonight for unwed mothers, as if I didn't have enough on my plate."

"You're on for Thanksgiving aren't you? You can bring your friend, the one—"

"That's over. His wife shipped his dog back. She got an apartment, no pets allowed."

"Oh, Jessie, I'm sorry."

The nurse laughed. "Don't be. He asked me to spend last weekend with him. I did. The first strike against him was he wanted me to tidy his house and iron his shirts. The second was the dog slept between us. In my ballgame, two strikes and you're out. So, yes, I'll be up for Thanksgiving, because I won't be around Christmas. I've booked myself on a cruise to the Bahamas."

"That's wonderful!" Kaley frowned. "You're deserting me!"

"Kaley, my friend, you have the patina of a woman in love. Don't begrudge me a tan." She lowered her voice. "And maybe a little dirty dancin' on the side. Cha cha cha."

"SLATER, you're not listening."

He put his finger on the survey grid of Rutledge land to hold his place. "I'm trying to plot how much fencing I need, missy. It's late. You're supposed to be in bed."

"Miss Henderson wants to know if you'll come and talk at fourth-grade assembly."

"No, go back to bed."

Lacy came around the table and faced him. "You have to," she said vehemently.

"Have to?" He threw down his pencil. "You're in trouble again. Who'd you have a fight with this time?"

"Nobody," she said truculently.

"Am I going to get a phone call from this nobody's parents?" It seemed to him the phone lines had no more than gone up when the phone had begun to ring with irate mothers of other students complaining that Lacy had hit, spit or used bad language toward their precious darlings. If he wasn't waiting for a call from Aunt Willie alerting him when she'd be up to traveling, he'd yank the damned thing out.

Lacy lowered her lids and pursed her lips as she did when she was indignant or disgusted. "They don't believe me."

"Who doesn't believe you? About what?"

"The kids at school," she said in an altered voice. "About you."

"Me?" He flared. "What have—"

"They don't believe you went all over Australia or found gold and opals, or almost died in the desert or sewed up your ownself—or anything. They think I'm lying, that I'm makin' you up because I don't have a daddy anymore. So you have to come to school and tell them."

"Miss Henderson knows I'm real. We've talked often enough."

"The kids don't," she retorted bluntly. "They laugh at me."

"You're a Rutledge. Laugh back."

"So you won't come?"

"I'm not parading myself in front of a bunch of fourth graders to get you off the hook. Stop boasting."

"Did you do all those things you told us about?"

"Yes, now go to bed."

"Then, I haven't been boasting."

"Fine. Just keep your mouth shut from here on out."

"I hate you," she said in an angry gulp. "You're not like my daddy. He would've come."

She fled the room.

Slater sat there a moment, then sighed absently as he rousted himself and followed Lacy. He'd come to the immutable conclusion that the best way to populate the earth was to clone adults.

The Mickey Mouse night-light was aglow, casting just enough brightness for him to negotiate toys and books and clothes scattered on the floor. Most of which were Lacy's. Jason piled all he owned in his bed and slept with it.

Lacy was stretched out stiff as a corpse. He sat on the side of her bed. "I know you're not asleep."

"So?"

"So, maybe after I finish Aunt Willie's room, I'll come over to the school."

Lacy sat up. "When will that be?"

"A couple of weeks."

She flopped back.

"Meanwhile, you lay off the gab and things will ease up."

She jerked the covers over her head.

"That's the best I can do, you little twit."

Slater went into the living room, added wood to the fire, and lowered himself into one of the two old overstuffed chairs he'd discovered amid the debris in the barn. They begged recovering, but were surprisingly comfortable and they held his bulk.

The new wood caught, the fire flickered. He yawned. The days were too short and the nights too long. He sat there, falling under the spell of the mesmerizing flames. Thoughts of Kaley intruded, she was in the flames, dancing, teasing, beckoning. He tried to shift his eyes away from the captivating vision, but it was as if the very flames themselves were a reminder of need, want and regret. He stretched out his legs to accommodate the throbbing in his loins.

Is this what he was reduced to? he wondered, smothered in self-contempt. Dreaming of the woman he wanted instead of having her? He closed his eyes and felt as though he were floating, as though he had no past, no future, no fears, no worries, and little by little sleep overcame him.

KALEY SAT on her worktable Indian fashion and gazed about the empty drying shed. There was nothing left. She'd been stamping orders Sold Out for a week.

She felt lost, at loose ends. With so much spare time on her hands, she'd cleaned the house, straightened cupboards, caught up her ironing, repaired the loose board on the porch. The highlight of her day now was when the school bus let the children out and they came romping up the lane to spend an hour or two.

She didn't even have aggravation and exaspertion to keep her company. Independent was so wrapped up in concern for Flossie that he'd lost interest in tormenting her.

She had not felt so vulnerable and insecure since her husband had died. She needed a warm touch, a hug.

She needed Slater Rutledge.

She got off the table and made her way to the barn. Though a slight wind kept the air chilly, the early-morning sun was bright and warm. The first snowfall of the year had melted away, leaving the ground windswept and damp, evergreens unadorned.

Kaley tugged her knit cap down over her ears and jammed her hands into her pockets.

She found Independent walking Flossie around the small corral out back and called to him. Flossie flattened her ears.

"Get outta here," he yelped. "You'll put her in a bad mood."

"I'm going for a walk."

"Well, go," he grumbled, and went back to cooing in Flossie's ear.

Kaley had become used to the sound of sawing and hammering reverberating down the mountain, but it was quiet as she approached the Rutledge homestead. Too quiet. Her heart skipped a beat. Perhaps Slater was ill again. As she skirted the stand of boulders that marked the path to his front door, she saw the reason.

Slater was taking advantage of the break in winter weather by giving the old place a fresh coat of paint. He had an eye for contrast, too. Window frames were the color of thick summer foliage, the clapboards a soft willow green.

She stopped and watched him for a few moments. He was hatless, his hair tied back, flannel shirt tucked into jeans, sleeves rolled to elbows. The sun caught the edge of his jaw and spilled onto the dark hair on his chest where it curled above the open neck of his shirt. There was a hushed stillness in the forest around her, an electric tension that seemed rooted in her loins.

Would there ever come a time, she wondered, when the width of his shoulders didn't take her breath away?

"This is good wholesome work, if you're looking for a job," he said without turning around.

Kaley went up onto the porch. "How do you do that?"

"I dip the brush in the paint—"

"How can you tell I'm here?"

"I heard you and smelled you."

"For how long?"

"Five minutes back maybe." He laid the brush across the top of the can and wiped his hands on a rag. He still wasn't looking at her.

"Slater."

"I'll make us a cup of tea."

"I can't go on like this. I've learned something about myself. I've always thought I had the patience of Job. I don't. When I told you I could wait, I was fooling myself. I wish I could undo the way I feel, but I can't." The tone of her voice changed, deepened. "I find I can't wait after all."

Slater felt a burn behind his breastbone. "I'll only be a minute. Sit on the steps."

"I don't want to sit on the steps." She wet her lips, went on hoarsely. "I don't want tea, or coffee or conversation. I want *you.* If it won't work after that, then it won't. It's really rotten of you to decide for both of us without...without..." She couldn't get another word out. She just stood there, barely able to breathe.

He looked at her, looked away, seeing the landscape but not seeing, his heart thudding like a herd of elephants stampeding while his soul turned inside out.

"I can't promise you a future, Kaley."

She moved closer, drawn by the subtle scent of soap, the laundered smell of his shirt. "I'm only asking for *now.*" She dropped her eyes and saw the bulge in his jeans. She lifted her face to him. "I dream of you every night, touch myself where you touched me, but it's not the same. I'm sick to death of being celibate."

She was offering him escape, temporary oblivion. He couldn't scrape from his mind the image of her on her knees in his bed, her head thrown back, the creamy column of her neck as she had arched against his hand. The yearning in his body went beyond the sexual, steering him into unsafe areas. He heard himself say, "It's ten o'clock in the morning, missy."

"So?" she wailed softly.

"Something like this might take all day."

Her eyes widened, her voice came barely audible. "You're saying yes? *Yes?*"

"There are limits to the amount of sexual attention a man can comfortably absorb. I went past my limit five minutes into our first meeting."

"A woman, too. I ache all over."

Their eyes held and they watched each other. He opened the door for her and she entered the house, walking backward into its warmth because she was terrified that if she took her eyes from him, he would change his mind or joke that he was teasing or merely disappear.

He reached for her, tugging the knit cap from her head, allowing her hair to spill over her shoulders. He bent to kiss the nape of her neck, and Kaley nearly swooned as she felt blood rushing to her face.

Sunlight crept around the naked oak sentry and poured into the bedroom through the bank of windows. Slater's bed was neatly made with new linens. She noted the addition of man-size pillows. But then Slater bent his head and kissed her lips, and she entered a shadowy cave of sensations felt only in her breasts and her stomach.

He began to undress her, discovering layers of shirt and undershirt and camisole and lace-up boots. "You're dressed for the weather," he observed, surprised. "You didn't plan this seduction?"

"I was only out for a walk. My boots aren't double-knotted. Let me. You're too slow."

He was smiling, nearly laughing, shaking his head as she stripped herself down to underpants, camisole and boots. "Good crying damn, you look like Sheena, the jungle girl." He pulled her along onto the bed until they were lying face-to-face, breathing each other's warmly scented breath.

"My boots..."

"Later," he choked. "I think I'm going to explode if we don't make love in the next ten seconds." He freed himself, pulled her panties aside and as he slipped his fingers into her, he let out his breath. "You're wet."

Kaley gasped, feeling herself throbbing where he touched her, moaning when he drew his hand away and spread her knees; slipping her panties off, he thrust into her and she heard his quick intake of breath. His hands were on her hips, drawing her into a rhythm as ancient as the mountain surrounding them. The fabric of his jeans was rough against her inner thighs. As he pressed deeper into her, she slipped her hands beneath his shirt and ran her fingers up the hard muscles of his back. He moaned, his breath caught somewhere in his throat.

He lifted her hips, her body spun out of control and he thrust deeper. Kaley breathed with her mouth open, pulling in the warm sunlit air. She felt him shudder and go still.

She gasped, near to tears as every cell in her body protested. "You didn't wait for me..."

"Poor missy," he murmured. "Let me help you catch up." A moment later he was nibbling on her nipples through the camisole as he gradually tugged it up and over her head.

"I want my boots off."

"Certainly," he said agreeably. But it took him an hour to get to her feet.

KALEY SAT astraddle of him, impaled and satiated. Slater's hands cupped her swollen and tender breasts. The sun was slanting westward, withdrawing its light, leaving thick shadows lying along the windowsills. It hadn't got past him that they'd made love time and again with no protection. His seed could be planting itself in her womb at this very minute. "Are you on the pill?"

Kaley shook her head. "Not since Virgil died. It didn't seem necessary. I'm not going to trick you into anything, if that's what's worrying you."

"All the same, if you miss your period, I want to know."

"I wouldn't keep something like that from you, but I didn't get pregnant today. It's not the right time in my cycle."

He was about to tell her he wanted to make love again, but he stopped himself. "The kids will be getting off the school bus soon."

"I know." Reluctantly she moved off him and began searching for her clothes, putting on whatever she found as she laid hands on it. "We wrecked your bed."

"That we did," he said smiling, but in the next instant his forehead was lined with a frown.

She felt sad that reality was so quickly creeping into this perfect day. "Are you angry with me?"

"With myself. I had no right to take so much of you."

"You didn't *take.* I *gave.* Are you going to manufacture an argument now just so I'll stay away?"

"Would it work?" He watched her wet her lips, watched how quickly her eyes filled with mischief.

"Not a chance."

He gave her a concessionary smile. "Didn't think so." He threw his legs over the side of the bed, found his jeans and stepped into them.

Kaley went over to him, folded him into a tight embrace and buried her face in his chest. "No matter what happens between us from now on, thank you for today." She looked up into his eyes. "So you don't have to wonder about it, I love you. Stop looking so morbid. Stick it in your ear, for all I care."

He held her at arm's length. "Don't say another word. You aren't being realistic."

"I don't have to be realistic. Especially not after I've just had marathon sex and my legs are so wobbly I may have to crawl down the mountain to get home."

"I'll drive you."

"No, I want time to myself between here and there. Did you see the doctor?"

His stomach contracted with such sudden force he thought it must show in his face. "What doctor?"

"The one Jessie suggested."

He exhaled. "Sure."

"And?"

"Like I said, a little American bacteria." Specifically the man had diagnosed a bone-marrow infection, probably stemming from unattended bruises, which was apparently the bane of unpadded and unskilled skateboarders, or so the doctor had informed him. The infection accounted for his aching limbs, but it wasn't life-threatening and had nothing to do with his other problem. Which he did not bring to the physician's attention. "I'm taking antibiotics like a good little boy."

He turned away from her to zip and snap his jeans. There was something unfamiliar in his face, like a man being sucked into quicksand, a powerlessness so alien to his demeanor that for an instant he looked like a different man, and Kaley felt a chill race down her spine.

He sat on the topsy-turvy bed to pull on his socks and boots.

"Whatever it is, Slater, I don't want to know."

He looked up sharply. "What're you nattering about now, missy?"

"You. When I took my marriage vows, it was until death do us part. I thought it would be *my* death and Virgil would have to go on without me. But of course, that was selfish and not how it was at all. So, whatever's wrong with you, I don't want to know. I don't want the pain of knowing."

He masked it expertly, but she saw telltale relief sweep over him as if he'd been given a reprieve, and his face took on such color that Kaley suspected he didn't even notice it in hers. So there was something! Her heart galloped. To detract him from her own trembling, she stretched her body, lithe and catlike. Then placing her hands on her hips, she sniffed. "In any case, I only came over to invite all of you for Thanksgiving. Come early in the afternoon. You can help stuff the turkey."

He looked from her to the bed and back again. "I like your way of issuing invitations, missy. Indeed I do."

She smiled, feeling a tenderness for him that was new. "Hold me a moment before I go?"

He took her into his arms, burying his face in her hair while a sinking feeling lay heavily in the pit of his stomach.

He was right all along. His want and need of her was going to be worse now than ever.

The trap he'd got himself into was entirely clear to him.

Chapter Eleven

"Can we go now?" Jason pleaded, anxious to get on the path. "Kaley said if we got there in time we could watch the Thanksgiving parade on television. Santa Claus is gonna be in it."

Slater stood back to admire his nephew. He was getting pretty damned good at parenting, if he said so himself. The boy's hair was brushed, his shirt tucked in, his socks matched and his shoes were laced without skipping a loop. "You're as ready as I can get you. Go."

"Just what're we supposed to tell Kaley about why you're not coming?" Lacy asked, moving off the side of her bed as if newly released from prison.

Slater felt as if someone had squeezed his heart. Lacy was remaining firmly entrenched behind a layer of hostility in an effort to manipulate him into her fourth-grade assembly. "Tell her I'm snowed under with work around here."

He walked a short distance down the path to see them safely on their way, then turned back.

Had he gone another yard, he knew he would've kept on, unable to stifle the seductive urge to see Kaley and hold her in his arms.

His thighs tightened reflexively.

If he closed his eyes he could feel her, smell her, taste her.

Part of him was still in awe of how she had allowed her entire being to be accessible to him. He looked back now with something almost akin to shame at their first greedy and frantic coupling. His doing. But the second had been so tender, he'd almost shed tears. Later they'd turned provocative and playful, and finally they'd made love in such an idyllic manner he felt they moved in slow motion. And perhaps they had, for he'd had time to record every touch, every move, every sensation.

He'd gone to sleep that night, free of anything other than a supple tiredness and wonderful dreams.

The children's chattering faded as they moved farther away. He looked up from his thoughts into the immense quiet to find himself standing in the yard facing his house.

The old place was taking on the air of home. His roots were making themselves felt. Aunt Willie had wanted him to get back to them, to stop his wandering ways.

He wondered what she'd say when he told her that he had one more journey to make, that he was up for an adventure that required no passport, no ticket, no map.

"WHAT DID HE SAY?" Disbelief etched Kaley's face as she quizzed Lacy for the second time.

Lacy shrugged. "He's got work to do. Are you gonna let us stay?"

"Of course you can stay. The parade's on. Go watch it with Jason, I'll make you both hot chocolate."

Kaley hurried into the kitchen where Jessie was sitting at the table reading the newspaper. "Slater is delayed." She kept her tone conversational. "Would you mind keeping an eye on the kids while I go see what's holding him up?"

"I don't mind a bit, but I'm not deaf. I heard Lacy say he wasn't coming."

"He will, he just needs to be talked into it. He's as stubborn as Independent."

"Well, I don't see him here, either. Seems to me you've struck out with all the men in your life."

"One of the reasons why I like you so much, Jessie, is that you're so wonderfully charming and sympathetic."

"I just hate to see you running after a man who so obviously doesn't want to be caught. You aren't being objective."

A shadow of impatience flickered in Kaley's eyes. She lowered her voice. "For your information, we spent all day in bed together day before yesterday. It was right for me and right for him. So don't tell me I'm not being objective. This is a matter of principle."

Jessie's mouth dropped open.

Immensely satisfied with her friend's reaction, Kaley grabbed her car keys from a hook and reached for her jacket.

"I promised the kids hot chocolate."

Jessie came to her wits. "God. How was it?"

"Incredible. Eat your heart out."

"Kaley Jackson, you astound me."

"Make that hot chocolate, okay?"

"I'll do it on the condition that you tell all." But she was talking to herself. Kaley was out the door.

"I JUST DON'T THINK it's a good idea, missy." He feasted his eyes on her. She wore dark slacks and a mauve-colored sweater that highlighted the color in her cheeks. Wisps of hair fell down her neck, fugitives from the pins holding it atop her head.

Kaley all but stomped her foot. "Then why didn't you decline my invitation day before yesterday? I have mountains of food prepared."

His soft laughter had a bitter edge. "You don't expect a man to think straight after a day like that, do you?"

"You always think straight."

"I'm not made of steel, Kaley."

She tried another tack. "I'll be miserable sitting down to Thanksgiving dinner knowing you're up her alone. Eating beans, probably."

"I told you there was no future with me. Leave it at that."

She shook her head in bewilderment. "You started this, dammit. We made love, Slater. Doesn't that count for anything?"

Bloody hell. "I'm backpedaling, missy. Face it."

"I won't. Why should I be any less stubborn and hardheaded than you?"

"Because you'll get hurt," he said gently.

"I'm hurting now. Are you sure you don't have a wife stowed away somewhere?"

He laughed.

She stared at him uncertainly. She was unnerved by the fact that she'd played her trump card with Slater and lost. But no, that couldn't be. Too often she doubted herself, or gave in against her better judgment. Every feeling she had for him, he'd returned. She had not been left wanting. Even now she could see the war in his face between desire and...well, that was the problem—*and what?*

"There has to be a reason you're backpedaling."

He took a long time answering and made up the lie that might have been true two months ago, but made him heartsick today. "The long and short of it is that I'm not the marrying kind, Kaley. I can feel your net closing in on me. Being kind to the kids, cooking meals, sex..." He shook his head. "I'm not ready to settle down. There's a lot of the world I haven't seen."

Something in Kaley begged her surrender, but she just couldn't. She gave an awkward little laugh, free of guile. "I didn't ask you to marry me, y'know. I only asked you to Thanksgiving dinner."

"My mistake."

She turned to go, stopped and looked back at him. "Do you regret making love to me?"

"Go home, Kaley."

"Well, I don't," she said, lifting her chin, looking at him in a way that made him suddenly overheated. "You know what I think? What I've thought all along? That you're trying to spare me from something. You've come home, Slater. Think about that. You could've just as easily taken care of Lacy and Jason in Atlanta until Aunt Willie recovered from her broken leg. It may have been Aunt Willie who suggested Crosswind Ridge, but it fit your plans." She took a wobbly breath. "I love you. I would love you if your ears fell off or your teeth fell out or if you only had one leg—anything. You'll keep that in mind won't you?"

He was staggered by her passion. A wave of emotion thickened his voice. "I will."

"Good."

She gazed at him with despair in her heart, knowing that whatever happened between them in the future was up to him. "When the children head home I'll send you a plate." She tilted her head, looking beyond him at the ramshackle house he'd turned into a snug retreat amid silvering trees and dead leaves. "It's tranquil up here today."

"Good thinking weather."

Her eyes smiled. "Yes, it is. So, do some."

He let out a long breath as she drove away, clipping the wild shrubs on the narrow zigzagging dirt lane. He looked down at his hands. They were shaking.

Unconditional love. That was the gift Kaley offered him, a gift unlike any he'd ever been given.

And he knew he did not have the right to accept her consistent bounty of affection without telling her of his medical condition.

He was on the debit side now.

It hurt him more somehow that the revelation would cause her pain.

Swallowing a hard knot of anger at his own helplessness, he turned his face up to the pale cold sunshine and railed at a silent God.

KALEY STARED at Independent in horrified dismay. "You can't do that!"

"I ain't askin' your permission. I'm tellin' ye. I'm takin' my mule up to the top of the mountain. If I hold off any longer she'll die in the barn and I ain't about to carve her up and bury her in parts. It ain't dignified. She's been a good mule and deserves what's fittin'."

Kaley stood up so hurriedly she knocked over her chair. "It's winter out there, you stupid old coot! That rain is going to turn to sleet. You'll die of cold or catch pneumonia—"

"Don't be callin' me names. I reckon I know winter from summer, wet from dry."

"You could break your hip again."

"Eh? Better there than here. I don't aim for you to fetch my drawers for me ever again."

Kaley burst into tears. "Don't go. Call a vet, please. You're all I have left. I'll worry myself sick. Suppose you die along with Flossie?"

He snorted. "Then you'll have the old place to yourself, lessen you keep lettin' Rutledge spawn run wild over it."

Kaley sobbed anew. That was another thing keeping her in a state of high anxiety. Slater was avoiding her. She had to ferret out what he was doing, how he was feeling, what he was thinking, by pumping Lacy and Jason.

"Shut your face, girl." Independent agitated around her. "I never could abide a woman's waterworks." He righted her chair and pushed her down on it. "I'm not some young sapling what can't take care of myself. Anyways, there's a fair-size cave up there. We use to boil down liquor in it. Flossie an' I will be snug as goose down."

Kaley sniffed. "But how will I know that?"

"Why, same as Sary use to. On fair days you can spot my cook fire of a mornin'. Now if you don't mind, I'd like them shotgun shells you hid from me."

"Why? What're you going to shoot?"

"A bear if I get hongry, a Rutledge iffen I don't."

Kaley blew her nose. "No way. Go without your gun."

Independent looked at her through his rheumy old eyes, his mouth downturned. "Can't," he said, his voice raspy. "Flossie might need some help gettin' from here to mule heaven."

Kaley closed her eyes and shuddered. "Bottom left-hand drawer of the bathroom cabinet."

Independent got to the hall and stopped. "Bottom left-hand drawer? Ain't that where you keep your personals?"

Kaley opened her eyes to find him flushed with embarrassment. "If you've got the stamina to hike up Crosswind Ridge in the dead of winter, old man, you ought to have the wherewithal to riffle a box of Kotex."

His blush deepened. "Girl, you ain't got the dignity God gave spit."

"Well, I don't need it, do I?" She sniffed. "I'm a Jackson."

"Make yourself useful then. Fill my poke with victuals."

"To last how long?"

"A week mayhap."

"A *week!*"

"Mayhap longer. I don't aim to rush Flossie."

"Oh, dear God. I'm going with you."

A frown bracketed his mouth. "She's my mule. I got to do this on my own. Anyways, come to the end, you'll go to pieces."

They were both reminded of her collapse and hysteria when Virgil died. She hated to admit it, but she knew Independent was right. She went over to him and put her arms around him. "Promise me you'll be careful."

"Hey!" he sputtered. "Quit that!" He jiggled his shoulders, squirming out of her grasp. "Gor! Never could abide that kissy-kissy stuff."

She stared him down. "Promise me you'll be careful or I'll kiss you smack on the lips."

"Lord love us." He backstepped. "You got my word. Now keep your distance."

An hour later she stood in the yard in her slicker as Independent led Flossie out of the barn into the gray mist. He raised his hand. She did the same.

You old softie, she thought, calling out, "Goodbye, Flossie."

The old mule looked her way; her ears went flat and she kicked out her hind legs, whiplashing the light pack across her haunches.

"Same to you, old girl," she replied, relieved to see Flossie still had a bit of grit and gumption, hoping it was enough to get her up the mountain. But then she remembered that Flossie wouldn't be coming back down and hot tears threatened to erupt.

She followed the pair as far as the graveyard, stopping when they disappeared into the forest, Flossie clip-clopping, Independent with his peculiar hip-shot gait. Then she sat on Virgil's grave, listening for Flossie's bell until it was lost in the hushed sound of raindrops plopping on the headstones.

She pulled a frost-killed weed from the dirt at her side, indignant at finding a weed there at all.

It was the living who suffered, she thought. It was the living who suffered and grieved and mourned and who felt so utterly alone.

SLATER SAT ACROSS from the old doctor, feeling like the worst fool in Fentress County. His only consolation was that the man wasn't laughing at him. In fact, he was angry.

"That was a stupid thing to do, young man. When I asked for your medical history, I expected you to be honest. I could've prescribed something that could've made you worse."

"You're positive the antibiotic isn't having an effect?" Since he'd been taking it, he hadn't had blurred vision and his headaches had been mild to nonexistent.

"Son," Doc Fuller said tiredly. "I wish I could say yes, but that antibiotic won't do diddly for a brain tumor, benign or otherwise."

Slater stood up. "Sorry I wasted your time."

"Not a waste, you're gonna pay me—I hope. Now, sit back down, and let's sort this out."

"What's to sort?" But Slater lowered himself into the tired old leather chair once again.

"I'm no neurologist, but if symptoms are disappearing, then perhaps the tumor is shrinking."

Slater let his breath out slowly. "On its own?"

"On its own, God's help or the devil's. Nothing surprises me in this business anymore. But if it's something you're doing, you want to do more of it."

"Like praying?" The words came out coated in sarcasm.

The doctor grinned, revealing a wide gap between his two front teeth. "Never have come across anybody cured with prayer. Saw hate cure cancer once, though. Seems like it just filled that old sourass up until he squeezed the cancer right out. Come to think of it, saw love do pretty near the same thing a few years back. A young girl, most hopeless case of lung congestion and pneumonia I ever did treat. She died on me twice, came back both times. Said she had to. She was getting married in two months to the man of her dreams and wasn't about to trade in her wedding dress for a shroud.'' The old doctor sighed. ''Well, I see I'm not impressing you. What're you doing different lately as opposed to three months ago? That is, besides mistreating your shin with an ax head and coming down with a bone-marrow infection.''

Slater twirled his hat in his fingertips and, because he was pissed at himself for having hope when he knew damned well there was none, he said, ''Having sex.''

The doctor's eyebrow shot up. ''Now, there's a thought. I always found sex draining myself. On the other hand, there's some that swear it stimulates dopaminergic neurons into releasing chemicals in the brain. Makes us feel good.'' He dropped his eyes to the notes he'd made. ''You willing to go over to the hospital and have some X rays made? I got a friend up to Nashville who's an ace in neuropathology.''

''A waste of time. I already know what my chances are with surgery.''

''No, no. I mean to just send him your X rays. He's no surgeon, but I'd swear he can look at pictures of a brain and tell you what you were thinking two weeks ago.''

''To what end?''

Doc Fuller shrugged. ''I don't know, son. But a look see won't hurt nothing but your pocketbook. The human body is a fascinating project. It don't do to discount it. Was me, I'd want to know for sure whether or not I had a reprieve from a death sentence.''

Slater sat there a moment, scared to hope and thinking of Aunt Willie, Jason and Lacy, the farm—

and finally, Kaley. He nodded. "I'll do it." He rose to his feet. "I wouldn't want Jessie Lukazewski, the county nurse to get wind of this."

Fuller snorted. "Praise be, I stay as far away from that do-gooder as I can. I haven't made the price of fish bait off her referrals. Speaking of fees, you just go on out to the front and pay Mrs. Fuller while I call over to the hospital and get you set up."

"How much?"

Doc Fuller eyed him from hat to boot. "You real solvent or just middlin'?"

Slater's eyes laughed. "Just middlin'."

"Twenty dollars," Fuller said loudly so it could be heard clear to the front of the office. Then he lowered his voice to a rusty whisper. "And I wouldn't mind if you offered me one of those cigars sticking outta your coat pocket."

By the time the x-raying was behind him and he came out of the hospital, the first patters of rain were rhythmically dropping from the sky. He could kill time in town for a few hours and pick up the kids from school, saving them a bus ride, or he could pick up a six-pack and go along home. But the kids liked riding the bus and he didn't want to put himself in the path of Miss Henderson.

He opted for home, a six-pack and a blazing fire. Kaley had a way of coming to him out of the flickering flames. He could do with an easy afternoon of daydreaming.

What he could do without were ideas and hope and cures and possibilities.

He considered the X rays an exercise in futility and humoring an old man.

He slowed as he drove up the switchback past the Jacksons. He didn't expect to get a glimpse of Kaley, not out in the rain, but he'd gotten used to rubber-necking each time he passed the place. He saw the figure sitting in the cemetery, the yellow slicker a bright flash of color against the gray landscape.

It was Kaley. He recognized her green knit cap.

He braked, but she seemed not to hear. She looked so small and alone sitting up there in the mist, it immediately crushed his urge to honk the horn and announce himself. He cut the motor, adjusted his hat brim and palmed the six-pack. The real thing was far better than a vision in the flames.

He walked across the yard and past the house and barn, expecting with every step that she would look up so he kept a smile on his face.

"You make it a habit to sit in boneyards in the rain?"

"Slater!" Her voice lifted in delighted surprise, contradicting the caution in her eyes.

He folded himself down beside her and dropped the beer between his knees. Almost at once the cold dampness seeped through his jeans. "Always thought it was disrespectful to sit or walk on a grave."

"I don't think old ghosts mind the company. Independent took Flossie up to a cave to die. He may have to shoot her."

Slater flinched. "Always a tough call."

"This is as far as I got following them. He's almost eighty and I guess Flossie is, too, in mule years."

"He'll be all right, I suspect. These mountains breed tough old coots. Want a beer?"

She started to refuse. It was crazy to sit out here drinking beer in rain turning to sleet when there was a perfectly warm house a few yards away, but she noticed there were fine lines around his gray eyes, and the muscles in his jaw were tensed, hinting that there was some struggle going on beneath the surface. "Okay."

He popped the tops and passed her a can. Kaley took a sip. "Are you just passing by or come for a neighborly visit?"

He drew a line in the moisture on his can with a fingernail. "I want to sit in front of a roaring fire and hold you for a while. Is that a pass by or a neighborly visit?"

Her intake of breath was a puff of noiseless air. "Sounds neighborly to me."

He finished off his beer, crushed the can and put it in his jacket pocket. "I need to tell you something, missy."

She looked at him expectantly.

"My ass is freezing."

"YOU'VE TURNED this place into a Christmas fairyland," Slater said, standing with his backside to the fire.

"I just used up the bits and pieces of stock too messed up to sell." She handed him a towel, and sat to exchange her wet boots for fleece-lined booties.

Slater dried his face and tossed the towel in her lap. "Is that comment supposed to make me feel guilty?"

"Well—if the shoe fits..." She looked up at him, her face softened with a smile. "Don't mind me. I feel a little out of it. You're beginning to steam. Want me to put your jeans in the dryer?"

He broadsided her with a look.

"I guess that's no. Would you like to see what I found in the barn?" She retrieved a wooden box from the cupboard and held out to him a handful of tree trinkets. "All hand-carved. They need washing and repainting, but I'm going to let Lacy and Jason do that. That is, if you don't have any objection."

"No objection," he said, first admiring a perfectly rendered deer, then a World War One doughboy. "You have to hand it to those old-timers. They sure had a way with a carving knife."

He arranged the trinkets in the palm of his hand and held them out to her. Kaley took them one by one, and when his palm was empty she held his hand for a moment, then bent her head and pressed her lips against the calluses.

"Ah, missy." There was very little left of his voice as he took her into his arms and buried his face in her damp hair, inhaling the scent of her.

She reached down, brushing her hand against his zipper.

He groaned softly, held her tightly for a long moment, then gently put her away from him. "We have to talk."

She gave a small shake of her head. "No, we don't. You sound as if you're going to tell me the world is coming to an end. We can just go on like this."

"Sorry, love, but we can't. *I* can't." He caught the shadow of fear in her eyes before she turned away to stare into the flames. "I've racked my brain about how and when to tell you, and came to the conclusion there will never be a good time, a right time."

Kaley put her hands to her ears and with a half-muted objection sank onto a foot stool. "I knew it. I always knew it."

He took her hands away from her ears and placed them in her lap.

She was suddenly very cold. Trembling, she sat forward, angling toward the fire so that he could not observe the fear in her face. *Calm, Kaley, calm.*

Slater lowered his bulk into the overstuffed chair behind her. It'd be easier this way, he thought, almost like talking to himself.

It was a moment before he spoke, and he began haltingly, but then the words flowed, far easier than he expected. "About a year ago I started having blurred vision . . ." He saw her shoulders tense.

"I put it down to all that glaring sun when I came up out of the mines. It didn't happen often, but often enough for me to take notice. A few weeks later, I started having headaches. On the whole, they weren't all that painful, just nagging, no worse really than a humdinger of a hangover. But the kicker came one afternoon when I went to sleep on one and didn't wake for two days. That scared me, losing two days. And I *thought* I was losing my mind. Going mad. That happened enough in the desert, not just to the miners but the women, too. I hied down to Adelaide and let the doctors have a look. A benign brain tumor. That didn't sound so bad.''

Kaley swallowed back the gasp that rose in her throat. She reached for a piece of split firewood and added it to the fire.

Slater emitted a sigh. ''It's where it's at that's the problem. Sort of midbrain, touchy to get in and out of with surgery and about a thousand things that can go wrong because there's only one right way.''

She looked back at him over her shoulder, the unvoiced question in her eyes.

''I've opted not to have the surgery.''

''But—''

He shook his head. ''The way it stands I've got a couple of good years on my side and perhaps a few not so good. Under the knife I could end up at worst, a vegetable, at best, perhaps having to learn to walk and talk and function all over again. Dead, I wouldn't be a burden to anyone, but they can't guarantee dead.''

''But there are all kinds of new science, laser surgery, and—''

''You're fighting it, missy. I'm not asking you to help me decide. That's done.''

Her head bobbed slowly. ''You came home from Australia to die.''

He could hear the devastation in her voice.

''I came home to rub my big brother's nose in my success. I suppose I came home to say goodbye, too. I planned on going back to Australia. But Jerome did a flyer, Aunt Willie broke her leg and I couldn't run out on her and the kids.''

Her eyes filled as she thought of what he'd endured this past year, what he endured every day. She folded her arms on her knees and laid her head down. She stayed that way a long time, until she felt Slater's fingertips tracing the ridge of her spine. A sick lump clogged her throat.

"What am I supposed to say?" She knew he would not tolerate pity, and he might misread compassion.

"Anything—or nothing."

There was just the slightest emphasis on "nothing," but Kaley was listening with a terrified heart and heard it.

"The first time I saw you I thought you were a Greek god rising out of that creek, or at the least, a Roman gladiator come to life. I was sure you were in my imagination, though. I thought I'd banged my head."

He smiled. "Not a Roman gladiator, missy. You'd never catch me in one of those girly togas."

Heart aching, she gave a superior sniff. "Nor a Greek god, either. It only took me a minute to get my wits back. Then I knew you were a lech."

He took his hand away from her neck. "And, now?"

"Oh, you're still a lech." Her voice ebbed away to a whisper. "Could I sit in your lap?"

He rearranged his long legs so that he could accommodate her. Kaley snuggled into the sanctuary of his arms and pulled back his shirt collar to press her lips against the taut cords of his neck. His skin was warm with the scent of soap and after-shave and tobacco. "You smell so good."

The long muscles of his arm tightened about her, and while one hand rested on her hip, the other circled her ankle, his thumb consciously or unconsciously—she couldn't tell which—massaged her Achilles tendon.

"Why wouldn't you let me harvest grapevines?"

"Because the land is mine. Jerome wanted to forget we came from rough stock. I paid the taxes every year. I was gathering Rutledge resources together. I didn't want Aunt Willie or the kids to have a problem with squatters after I left. It was better to establish boundaries up front. Besides that, I wasn't about to let some huffy little twit take advantage of me."

"Huffy little twit?" She nipped his earlobe with her teeth. "I resent that." She had to ask. "Are you still planning to go back to Australia?"

The rain pattered fitfully against the windows, the clock on the mantel tick-tocked and an occasional spray of wet shot down the chimney and hissed in the grate.

"There, or somewhere. When it's time."

Kaley's stomach lurched.

"There's a footnote," he said slowly, as if his hand on her ankle reminded him of something. "I saw Doc Fuller today and had some X rays taken. I thought the pain in my head abated because of the antibiotic he prescribed. The long and the short of it is that he's sending the prints to a colleague to see what's going on inside my skull."

"But the tumor is still there."

"Afraid so. The peculiar thing is, I haven't had a headache since we had sex."

Kaley shot straight up on his lap and stared at him, her irises dark as midnight. In the face of the horrible news he'd just dealt her, it didn't seem possible that she could smile, but all the same she felt the corners of her mouth lifting. "Truly?"

"True fact or coincidence."

"Gee." She leaned forward to press her lips against his chin, and began to unbutton his shirt, her fingers warm and silky where they met his skin.

Despite the intoxicating feel of her, Slater thought of the X rays and the ace neuropathologist in Nashville. He wondered if the gods were hatching some Machiavellian plot to give him hope before allowing the sword to slip its sheath and crush him altogether.

Kaley's hands stilled. "You've gone away from me." There was worry in her eyes. "Would you rather not?"

He took her hand and placed it at the juncture of his thighs. "Does that answer your question?"

"Dear me. And all this time I thought that was your hipbone."

He tilted her chin up. "You're taking this better than I expected."

"I hurt for you, Slater. I hurt for me. Would you prefer I get hysterical? I feel like it. I feel like Flossie has just kicked me in the stomach. I feel like crying or screaming. I want to push what you've just told me out of my mind and think it's not true. But I want to be brave, too." Her eyes welled with tears. "Only I don't feel brave. I feel lost. And angry. It's going to take getting used to." She dropped her head on his shoulder. "I know what the pain is like to lose someone I love. But I'd rather have the pain along with the love than neither. I know that much about myself."

"Hold on." He took her by her shoulders and held her face away from him. "I'm not talking about marriage. I won't marry you."

She looked at Slater in disbelief. "But, we could make wonderful use of your two good years. We could marry, I could have a baby, help you establish the horse farm. Jason and Lacy need mothering. Independent will give up on his silly feuding once he learns—"

He shook her roughly. "Stop. That's not the kind of hand we've been dealt."

She swallowed. "Wait a minute." The anger surfaced. "You mean you want us to love, but on your terms. No marriage, no babies? No business? You don't want sympathy. You've decided your fate. Where does that leave me? You don't have the right to decide my fate, too."

"That's why I told you, Kaley. I wanted to be fair."

"Fair! What's fair? I'm to be left alone again with nothing to hold on to? You've nearly put me out of business!" She scrambled from his lap. "You want to use me for sex and leave out everything else? What am I supposed to do? Live in limbo until you take yourself off to die somewhere?"

He came to his feet, eyes blazing. "I was playing this your way, Kaley. Hell, yes, I want you. I want to live as hard and fast as I can every day, every hour I've got coming. But I'm not going to end up a cripple or blind and expecting you to take care of me. Rutledge land has got to provide for Lacy's and Jason's future.

And knowing what I know, I don't have the right to marry and leave a son to tough it out on his own. I *hate* what Jerome has done to Jason and Lacy."

She shoved against his chest. "Don't yell at me."

He grabbed her wrists. "You don't seem to hear soft talk, missy. Fate has cut me off at the knees. What I feel for you ties me in knots, but I can't promise you diddly. That's the way it is."

The telephone rang, startling them both. Slater released her. Kaley snatched up the receiver. "Hello!"

"Kaley, dear? Did I catch you at a bad time?"

Consternation shot through her like a bullet. "Oh, Mother." She glanced at Slater. He was shrugging into his coat, his expression sphinxlike as he headed for the front door. "No," she said, squeezing her eyes shut. "It's not a bad time at all."

Chapter Twelve

"Are you sure nothing's wrong, dear? You sound overwrought."

"I'm concerned about Independent. He's—"

"It'd be nice if you'd have a little concern for your father, too."

Kaley clenched the receiver. "Is Dad okay?"

"He's fine. It's just we never hear from you. We miss you."

Kaley passed her hand through her hair. "I miss you, too. I'm looking forward to seeing you both."

There was a brief pause. "Well, that's why I called. I'm afraid we aren't going to be there for Christmas after all. A friend of your father's has invited us to Key West for the holidays and we've decided to accept. You don't mind, do you? You know I'd be bored in that provincial wasteland you call home these days."

The anger she felt for Slater was on the surface. Now she felt wounded on all fronts. "Actually, Mother, I think I do mind. You've never been here. You didn't even come for Virgil's funeral."

"We sent flowers."

"My husband died, Mother, and you weren't here for me." *Am I hearing myself correctly?* she thought, amazed as much at the tone of her words as their content.

"That was two years ago, for heaven's sake! We begged you not to run off and marry him, Kaley. Why are you being so hostile at this late date?" Her voice tightened. "Your father and I gave you everything money could buy—nice clothes, a good education—all the advantages, and the way you repay us is to begrudge us a nice holiday?"

Kaley felt so suddenly sad, her stomach twisted. "Of course, I want you to have a nice Christmas, Mother. I was just hoping you and Dad would have it here with me and Independent."

"I don't like the country—all those insects, no decent restaurants, no theater. You know that. I sometimes think that's why you're holed up there, just to spite me."

Kaley had the urge to defend herself, her life-style, but it came to her that Miram Sloan was so focused on herself that she'd twist and contort everything Kaley said until the attention was back on her. She realized Miram craved approval, was obsessed by it. As the daughter she was merely an extension of that craving.

"Living here is important to me, Mother. I can't really say why. But listen, perhaps in Key West you'll be able to wear your sequined cocktail dress."

She heard her mother's intake of breath. "Oh, I will. Richard is having a lovely dinner in our honor. I just wish you'd stop vegetating and come home. You'd feel so much better about yourself."

"Anything is possible, I suppose. Give my love to Dad. And—Merry Christmas to both of you."

"You too, dear. Hugs."

Gently Kaley replaced the receiver on the hook. "Hugs, to you too, Mom."

I wish I could please you. But I can't. All that's left is for me to please myself. Briefly the old insecurities surfaced, but she brushed them aside.

She walked over to the window and looked out. Slater's truck was no longer parked in the switchback.

The rain-splashed window gave back her reflection. She looked exhausted and frail, her hair in tangles.

And no wonder. Life was not exactly going as planned.

But then she met her own eyes in the glass. She saw depth there, and realized she had strengths that she had not even begun to tap.

"WE'RE HAVING your bon voyage supper in front of the fire," Kaley said to Jessie, arranging the foods on a tray. "I've even sprung for a bottle of champagne."

"Is it just us, then?" Jessie puzzled. "Slater isn't coming? Thelma Broom?"

"It's not polite to look a gift horse in the mouth, Jessie Lukazewski. Besides, we haven't done any girl talk in ages."

"What about Independent?"

"Still up on the ridge. I start my day every morning trying to separate his smoke from the vapors and clouds. Either Flossie is taking her time, or he's sitting up there on top of the mountain just to irritate me.''

They toasted away the champagne. Kaley picked at her food. Jessie sighed.

''Give with the girl talk. You've had another spat with Slater.''

Kaley bit her lip. The stakes were so high with Slater, she didn't want to voice her fears. She felt she had no hope of recapturing him. ''It's—my parents aren't coming for Christmas after all.''

Jessie reached out and put her hand over Kaley's. ''Oh, honey. I'm sorry.''

Kaley tilted her head and gazed into the fire. ''I don't think I am. A little hurt, maybe. I would've been tense the entire time they were here. Lacy and Jason are a big part of my life now, and Mother wouldn't be able to keep from criticizing them. Independent could stay out of her way, or give as good as he got, but the kids are fragile right now. This is their first Christmas without either of their parents. In the past, Aunt Willie apparently stood in at holidays and so forth, but Slater says she's having a terrible time. Until she's able to have a walking cast, he can't bring her up. Worse, I think, is there still hasn't been any word from the mother, Renie, and that's got Lacy in a blue funk.''

''You want to make it up to all of them. You want to be mother, father, lover, and angel of mercy all rolled into one.''

''You think so? Well, maybe I do—but not all at the same time.''

"You can't save the world. You can't keep other people from being hurt. You can't take their pain as your own."

"Don't worry about me. I'm enjoying this Christmas. Every morning I make the fire, toss on an apple and a handful of cinnamon, hum Christmas carols.... It feels wonderful."

"I'm going to come back from my holiday," Jessie lamented, unconvinced, "and find you a basket case."

"You will not! Anyway, what with Flossie coming to the end of her days, it's Independent we need to worry about."

"Wanna bed? Oops—Freudian slip."

Kaley laughed. "Too much champagne." She reached behind her chair and placed a gaily wrapped package in Jessie's lap. "Here, be opening this while I put on the coffee."

From the kitchen Kaley heard her friend snicker, then guffaw. Jessie came to the kitchen door with the card in her hand. "What the best-dressed man aboard ship wears? And a dozen, no less. You have higher hopes for my love life than I do. What in the world got you thinking so wicked?"

"You have twelve days of vacation so I just thought, hmm, one-a-day keeps the doctor away."

"Ain't it the truth!"

After they'd shared the coffee and Jessie drove off with the cheerful vow to come home with a tan to beat all tans, Kaley stood in the yard, her arms folded against the December chill.

The moon had risen high enough to drop small coins of silver light across the mountain, and the stars were crisp little diamonds in a blue-black sky. She wondered if it'd do any good to toss a wish into that twinkling vastness and expect it to land true.

Suddenly two stars fell, long silver trails gliding into the dark horizon. An omen! She closed her eyes and made her wish.

As she went back into the house to clear away glasses and dishes, she felt aglow. Perhaps the wine had a mellowing effect. She only knew that she wanted to take that feeling with her to bed.

She had all the dishes on the tray when the knock came. Fear caught her throat, her first thought being that Jessie had been too tipsy to drive, that she'd put the car in a ditch or hung it over a gully.

Cloaked with guilt, Kaley yanked open the door, fully expecting to find Jessie at her feet, bruised and bleeding.

"Whoa, missy. Who were you expecting? The bogeyman?"

Kaley was choked into silence while her brain made the adjustment from Jessie to Slater.

His face was drawn, his eyes unsmiling. "I'm having a miserable night."

Kaley found her voice. "The headaches have returned..."

"No. I keep seeing that look of devastation on your face when I lit out of here the other day. I go to sleep with it, wake up with it. And pretty soon the inside of your house is going to be as cold as it is out here."

"Oh. *Oh.*" She moved aside and closed the door once he'd stepped inside.

He took in the burning candles, the holly and pine on the mantel, the dishes and empty champagne bottle. He frowned. "You've had a party."

"Just Jessie. She's going on a cruise the end of next week. Tonight was the only night she could spare for a bon voyage supper. Slater, why are you here?"

He tensed, hoping they weren't headed for another fight. "I don't like knowing I hurt you." He leaned an elbow on the mantel.

Kaley sank into a chair. "It's not your fault. You warned me. And more than once. Let me take your jacket. You want some coffee? There's still—"

"No, thanks. I don't want to get too comfortable, not with the kids up to the house asleep. A grizzly might break in."

She gave a half smile. "You're the closest to a grizzly on Crosswind."

"Ah. Almost there, missy."

She looked up at him, her face so pale it looked translucent, her eyes rimmed with smoky lashes. "You expect me to believe you came over here at ten at night in forty degree weather for a *smile?*"

"That, and to make sure you were okay. I've had the feeling you've been dodging me."

"You left me with the impression you didn't want to see me."

"I very definitely left you with the wrong impression."

Kaley exhaled tremulously. "You were right about one thing,. The knowing *is* worse."

"If I had the power to make things different, I would."

"You haven't heard from Doc Fuller?"

"We talk. The ace neuropathologist is attending a symposium on the West Coast, not expected back until the twenty-third."

"What would it mean if he finds the tumor is shrinking?"

He walled her in with his eyes. "That'd be a whole other ball game."

"Do you feel lucky?"

"Right now is not a good time for me to feel anything."

"I could never cut myself off from my emotions that easily."

Suffused with a sense of disembodied helplessness, Slater looked down into the embers in the grate. "You're attributing to me more strength than I own, Kaley."

"You're stronger than I am."

He pursed his lips. "Not by much, right this minute. I'd better get along before I demonstrate just how weak-willed I am."

"Well this time I'm going to take you at your word." She tilted her head and smiled at him.

As if to seal the fragile peace treaty they'd created between them, Slater bent down and pressed cool lips to her forehead.

"When are you planning to buy stock for your homestead?" she asked, moving onto another topic because she didn't have the forbearance to continue the present one without making an utter fool of herself.

"Early spring. I'll hit some auctions, maybe go out west, see what the government is offering in wild mustangs."

"I want to get Independent a horse or mule or something to replace Flossie."

"I'll be glad to keep an eye out."

"I can't wait that long. I want it in the barn when he comes down, as a Christmas present." She was suddenly overcome with anguish. "You're making plans for the future, Slater. Why can't you include me in them?"

"I can leave a horse behind . . ." He stopped, groping for words that would describe what he thought of the situation. "I get one tomorrow at a time, missy."

She gave him a wry smile. "Isn't that all anyone gets?"

"I won't argue the point with you. I've spent most of the past couple of days thinking about us—and the possibilities. You want me to be a little more than I am—or perhaps, a little less."

"That's not true!" she said hotly. "You make me sound like my mother. She's always wanted me to be something I'm not, or marry a man that met her approval, speak several languages, be a mathematical whiz. I wouldn't ask you to be something you're not! Or more of what you are, or less! I know how it hurts to try to live camouflaged as something you're not."

"Whoa. I didn't mean to poke a hornet's nest, love. I want you in my life, but I won't let myself become an albatross around your neck." He moved away from the fireplace.

"*I* won't let you become an albatross!"

"You can't stop what's going on in my head, Kaley. You don't have the power to do that. No one does, unless it's God, and I don't think He's looking my way at the moment."

He put his hand on her chin and turned her face so she could not avoid his eyes. "If it makes you feel any better, I dream of you every night, I dream about what might have been, and I wake up every morning reaching for you."

She turned her face so that her mouth met the hard, toughened skin of his palm.

Her lips were soft and full and moist.

Resolutely Slater withdrew his hand before he succumbed to a seductive, treacherous hope. "I have to go. Jason sometimes wakes up from a bad dream. He'll be frightened if I'm not there."

"I'm frightened, too!"

"I know, but you're not five years old."

She sniffed. "I have bad dreams."

"Well, the next time you do, come see me. We'll talk about it."

"It'd be easier if I could just turn over in bed—"

He put a finger to her lips. "I ache for you, Kaley. Don't make it harder on me than it already is."

Discouraged, she trailed him to the door, her gaze on the width and breadth of his shoulders. The calves of his legs hugged the khaki pants he wore. An airy sensation lodged in her throat. "Slater," she whispered.

He turned, and at the look on her face, pressed his lips lightly to hers, lingering a moment to absorb their softness. "In case you doubt it," he murmured, "you turn me on, missy."

"Fat lot of good that does," she said crossly.

"It is good, keeps my spirits warm." His voice wafted over Kaley like a caress.

From the stoop, he looked back at her once, collecting her image to take to bed with him.

Chapter Thirteen

When Kaley got home from scouring Fentress County for "something live" for Independent, she found Lacy, looking glum and forsaken, sitting on her porch steps. The live thing she'd bought, after some dickering, was curled up asleep on the warm floorboard of the truck. She left it there for the moment and went to Lacy.

"What's up, sweetheart?"

To her consternation, Lacy's face screwed up, she bent her head into her hands and began to weep noisily. "She isn't coming. She's known all along that Daddy died and she isn't coming."

"Oh, Lacy." Full of aching pity for the child, Kaley sat on the stoop and put a consoling arm about her. It was long minutes before the worst of the sobbing subsided.

"I hate her! I just hate her. I hope she dies!"

"I know," Kaley crooned. "It hurts so bad you think nothing will ever make the pain go away."

Lacy wiped her nose on her sleeve. "We got a Christmas card, that's all. She's in Reno, Nevada, because there's a big card game and she can't come to see us. She has to stay with her husband because she's his luck. She said it was nice that Aunt Willie and Uncle Slater are taking care of us, because she lives in hotel rooms and that's not good for kids."

Kaley looked over at the truck. The dog had awakened, had climbed onto the seat and had her paws against the window. She was fat and scruffy-looking, a shepherd-hound mix, or so its previous owner had sworn. "The best coon-huntin' dawg in all of Fentress County."

Independent had not the slightest interest in coon hunting.

"My mother isn't coming for Christmas, either," Kaley said. "She's going to a party in Florida instead so she can wear her red sequined dress. I don't hate her, though. I just feel sad for her. I feel sad for your mother, too. She's missing out on knowing you, and you're a pretty nice person to know."

"Jason doesn't care at all. He says he doesn't have a mother."

Kaley gave a small laugh. "Well, he's a boy. What do boys know?"

Lacy lifted her head. "Not much. Except Slater. He knows a lot."

"Speaking of your uncle, does he know where you are?"

"He thinks I'm sulking in the barn."

"Let's go and call him."

Lacy trudged into the house behind her and slumped into a chair while she called Slater. He answered on the first ring.

"You must've been on top of the phone. It's Kaley."

"I thought it might be Doc Fuller."

She kept her tone neutral. "I won't keep you, then. Lacy's here with me."

"That rotter. Send her home."

"Not just yet, she's a bit melancholy." And because she knew Lacy was eavesdropping, she said, "She surprised me by being here when I got home, and now I don't have any way of getting her Christmas present into the house without her seeing it."

"You shouldn't—"

"So you don't mind if I go ahead and give it to her?"

"I don't—are we having the same conversation here?"

"Absolutely," Kaley said and hung up.

A glance out the corner of her eye told her Lacy was sitting up, almost dry-eyed, trying not to appear curious. She went to the fireplace, lighted the kindling, waiting while it caught. "How about a cup of cocoa? I've got to get the chill out of my bones."

"You bought me a Christmas present?" Lacy's voice was small and awed.

"More than one," Kaley told her, indicating the wrapped packages beneath the tree. "But this one is extra special. I was hoping to keep it secret until Christmas morning." She put forth her best sigh. "It might not suit you, though. You're kind of persnickety."

"I'm not."

Kaley gave her a look.

"Maybe I am—a little."

"Well, put your jacket back on. We'll get it out of the truck. But if you don't like it—"

"I will."

The dog was lying across the seat, but as soon as Kaley opened the truck door it leaped out, raced to the side of the house, emptied its bladder, then trotted back to where she and Lacy stood. Tail wagging, it sat and eyed them both with soulful brown eyes. Lacy was slack-jawed.

"You bought me a *dog?*"

"See if she'll come to you."

"What's her name?"

"She doesn't have an official name. The people who had her kept her penned up with their other dogs. She was the smallest, so I took her." She was also dirty and smelly.

"Here, doggie." Lacy clapped her hands. The dog inched forward.

"She's scared of me."

"She has to get used to you. It will help if you feed her. I'll go see what scraps are in the fridge."

Kaley took her time opening a package of weiners while watching out the kitchen window. Lacy sat on the cold ground, trying to coax the dog into her lap and inside her coat. When that didn't work, Lacy took the dog by its paws and pulled it onto her lap. Its tail began wagging like a whirlygig, and it licked excitedly at Lacy's chin. Lacy laughed.

Kaley waited another moment or two, then called Lacy inside. The dog followed, but halted at the threshold, reluctant to step across.

"I don't think she's ever been in a house. Maybe she'd like this." She passed a wiener to Lacy. "Once she's eaten, we'll give her a bath."

Thirty minutes later, after devouring the entire package of wieners and splashing around in the tub, the dog was wet and shivering, but reasonably clean and smelling of Kaley's bath salts. Kaley leaned back on her heels. "We should've put on aprons. We're both drenched."

"We can dry in front of the fire," Lacy said, continuing to vigorously dry the dog with one of Kaley's best towels. "I think I'm going to call her Georgia, because that's where I was born." She hugged the dog and, whispering "Georgia" into its ear repeatedly, she led her into the living room.

Kaley stayed behind to freshen the bathroom and rinse the dirt down the drain.

She leaned her elbows on the tub. Three days to Christmas. She wouldn't find another gift so right for Independent with time so short. On the other hand, Independent would be grieving for Flossie. Perhaps he would not be interested in shifting loyalties on the heels of Flossie's demise. In retrospect, the dog was small exchange for Flossie. And coming from her, Independent was as likely to ignore it as take to it.

It was Lacy who needed something to love and be loved unconditionally in return. She'd done the right thing.

In the living room, Lacy sat before the fire on the floor, Georgia on her back, allowing Lacy to scratch her tummy. "I'm pretty sure she likes me now."

Kaley sank in a chair and propped her feet on a footstool. ‘‘She'd be a dumb dog if she didn't. Like I said, you're easy to like.’’

Lacy kept her eyes on Georgia. ‘‘I guess I always knew Mother wasn't going to come.’’

Kaley leaned her head back and closed her eyes. She said softly. ‘‘Your mother doesn't see beyond herself, Lacy. She's so caught up with her own life, her own self, that she doesn't see you and Jason in yours. My mother is the same way. She never learned to reach outside herself.’’

‘‘Is that why you gave me Georgia? So I'd learn to reach outside myself? I was only thinking of myself when I learned she wasn't coming to get us.’’

‘‘No, I felt sorry for Georgia. She was in a pen with a bunch of big old dogs, and she looked at me with her big eyes and I just had to take her. If you didn't want her, I was going to keep her for myself.’’

‘‘She's the best Christmas present I ever got.’’

‘‘She's the best Christmas present I ever *gave.*’’

‘‘She's just mine—not Jason's?’’

‘‘Just yours.’’

‘‘Boy, just wait until Slater sees her.’’

Yes, Kaley thought, pondering his reaction. Just wait.

Lacy had a thought. ‘‘He might not let me keep her.’’

‘‘Yes, he will. Perhaps not in the house, but this is a good place for dogs.’’

Slater's reaction. Emitting an unconscious sigh, Kaley's thoughts galloped. Here she was moralizing about others when she was caught up and centered on herself. Slater had come to the end of his rope and was swinging on it. How selfish of her to try to force him to take on more than he could cope with or manage.

She looked up from her thoughts to find Lacy at her elbow, looking as troubled as she had an hour ago.

"What is it, sweetie?"

"Could I live with you?"

"It would be wonderful if we could figure a way, but I don't think Slater would like that."

"He might."

"Here, sit on my lap." Lacy took the perch stiffly. "You've had another fight at school."

"Worse."

Kaley put her arms about her thin waist, coming into contact with Lacy's tiny jutting bones. Georgia rolled over and cocked her head, watching them both. "Sometimes things aren't as bad as they seem. Tell me what happened."

"Well, you know the kids tease me." Kaley nodded. "They called me a liar because they don't believe Uncle Slater found gold and opals, and hunted horses in Australia."

"That's understandable, sweetheart. Slater was an adventurer. He's done things many people only dream about. Some of the things he's done are unimaginable even to me."

"But I told them I could *prove* he did."

"Oh. So that's why you wanted him to address fourth-grade assembly."

Lady nodded. "But he wouldn't do it. And then the kids dared me to prove it. Especially this one boy, Billy

Snow, only I call him Billy Snot.'' She exhaled wearily. ''So I did.''

''It sounds as if you solved your problem, then.''

Lacy's features creased in a frown, her hands braced rigidly on her knees. A few seconds passed. ''I lost Uncle Slater's opals and the big gold nugget.''

The back of Kaley's neck went prickly and cold. She recalled the chamois of rocks she'd found in Slater's chest while searching for medicine. Not rocks. Opals and gold. Good heavens.

''I didn't mean to,'' Lacy cried plaintively. ''I just took them out of his chest to show the kids and Miss Henderson. And when I got home from school, I didn't have them anymore. Now, school is out for the holidays, and if Uncle Slater looks in his chest and finds them gone, he'll kill me. I know he will. They were worth thousands and thousands of dollars. Maybe even a million.'' She gazed into Kaley's face. ''You won't tell him will you?''

Kaley did not want to undo the fragile bond of trust that was beginning to gel between them. ''I don't have to say anything right away. But if he discovers them gone, *you* are going to have to tell him.''

''I'm too scared.''

''Let's call Miss Broom and see what she has to say. Maybe the school custodian found them.''

Hope leaped into Lacy's face. ''But suppose one of the kids *stole* them from me? Uncle Slater was going to sell them to buy horses.''

Kaley did not want to think past calling Miss Broom.

"Oh, dear me," Miss Broom exclaimed after Kaley explained the situation. "I'll try to get in touch with Miss Henderson and the principal. I'll go over to the school myself first thing in the morning. They're worth thousands, you say?"

"I expect so."

"Whatever possessed that child to do something so unwise?"

"Pride," Kaley said.

"Of course. That does us in more often than not. It may take me a day or so to run down Miss Henderson. The last-minute Christmas rush keeps everybody in a dither."

"I don't suppose another day or two will make any difference." Her tone was sadly reflective. "I'd hate to see this ruin Christmas."

"It would put a damper on things. Have faith, dear. They may be sitting in lost and found right this minute. Just keep mum until I check and get back to you."

After she hung up, Kaley felt thoroughly unsettled, torn between keeping Lacy's trust and the knowledge that Slater had a right to know his opals were missing.

"Well?" Lacy asked, looking as if she were about to split wide open.

"Miss Broom is going over to the school tomorrow to see if they're in lost and found. She's going to get in touch with Miss Henderson. You don't have to say anything for now, but if the opals aren't found, you're going to have to own up."

Lacy went over and sat beside Georgia. She took a long deep breath. "I wish I hadn't done it now. I know he'll kill me."

"He won't do that, but you can expect him to be very, very unhappy." She couldn't even begin to imagine the repercussions.

Lacy laid her head down on Georgia's stomach. "If you won't let me come live with you, he'll probably put me in an orphanage."

"I don't think he'd let you off the hook that easily."

Lacy nuzzled her face into the dog's fur and began to cry again.

Consternation throbbed in the center of Kaley's chest. Why was everything going so wrong? The loss of his nest egg might well be the last straw for Slater.

Sniffling, Lacy sat up suddenly. "Georgia has two hearts! I can hear them. Come listen."

To humor her, Kaley knelt down and put her hand on the dog's chest. "One heartbeat."

"Not up there, down here."

Kaley ran her hand lightly over the dog's stomach. Loving the attention, Georgia stretched out even more. Kaley put her palm flat on the dog and left it there. She felt tiny, squiggling movements against her hand. "Uh-oh."

"What?" Lacy wondered, alarmed. "Is she sick? Is she all right?"

Kaley sighed. "She's going to have puppies."

The expression on Lacy's face was beatific. "When?"

"I don't know. Soon, I suspect. That's why she's so lethargic."

"Gosh. I'm going to be a mother. No, the owner of a mother." She whipped around and surprised Kaley by throwing her arms around her neck. "This is really and truly the best Christmas present ever!"

"I'm glad you're happy, sweetie." She disengaged Lacy's arms. "I never did make that cocoa. We'll have a cup, then I'll take you both home. I want a word with Slater, anyway."

Lacy huffed, her eyes alight with fear. "About the opals?"

"No, something else. We'll wait on the opals until we hear from Miss Broom. With any luck we might be able to squeak through the holidays without the world crashing down on top of us all."

When she pulled up in front of Slater's, he came out to meet them. He eyed the dog, the fierce grip Lacy had on it.

"Will it be okay?" Kaley asked him, a hollow feeling in her stomach.

"We already gave her a bath," Lacy put in.

"I won't mind a dog around the place."

He helped Lacy out of the truck and she went into the house, Georgia in her arms, calling for Jason.

Slater looked at Kaley. "Come in for a few minutes?"

Suddenly, Kaley felt like weeping, a sure sign of perversity. God, what was wrong with her? "Can I come back later? I didn't bank the fire."

He lifted an eyebrow. "How much later?"

"After the kids are in bed?"

"Sounds promising."

She averted her face. "You're positive it's okay about the dog. Lacy was so forlorn . . ."

"It's fine about the dog, missy."

She offered up a tenuous smile. "I'll walk over. About nine."

SHE DIDN'T HAVE TO KNOCK. He was sitting on the porch, smoking. He stood when she was within several yards of him and ground out the cigar beneath the heel of his boot.

"Chilly out," he said.

"Walking uphill kept me warm."

"Beer or brandy?" he asked, ushering her through the front door.

"Brandy. I could use a fortifier. As long as it's not Independent's."

He'd built up the fire. It crackled pleasantly. He'd also made a stab at decorating, and hadn't done too badly, Kaley thought. The Christmas tree, off in a far corner, was well lighted and hung with icicles and candy canes. Lying across the back of the sofa were two stockings, ready to be hung. Slater returned with a beer for himself and brandy for her, served in a juice glass. She took a small sip.

"You're not here to sing Christmas carols, missy. Spit it out."

"This is not as easy for me as I thought it'd be," she said inadequately. She had to choose her words with care. She couldn't say she couldn't live without him, because that was the crux of it.

"Sit down," he suggested, moving toward the sofa.

"No, you go ahead. I think better on my feet." He sat. She stood. It was a minor advantage, but Kaley was grateful for it. She cocked her head, listening for sounds inside the house. The crackling fire, the creak of the sofa as Slater settled himself, her heart beating in her ears. Nerves, she knew, and it was a moment before she realized she'd begun to speak aloud the thoughts that had been circling her mind for hours.

"I've been so unfair." She breathed slowly and deeply. "And, I've never been so frustrated in my life, because there's nothing I can do to help you or stop that thing from growing in your head. I can't *do* anything to make it better."

His smile was tender and mocking. "There's a definite undercurrent to his conversation, missy. Would you mind bringing it up so I can share it?"

"Don't rush me!" Her head felt top-heavy. Her mouth was too dry. Her stomach ached. She downed half the brandy left in her glass, feeling it sear its way down her throat. She got her breath back and forged ahead. "I told you that I'd love you no matter what. Then I got selfish. I wanted you to love me, but on my terms. I haven't been considering where you're at, the responsibilities you have. I haven't looked at things from your point of view. I've put you in the position of consoling me."

He put his beer can on the floor between his feet and took out a cigar, taking his time peeling it, biting off the end, lighting it. He stared up at her with an implacable face.

"Where are you taking this?" he asked, blowing smoke and watching it rise.

"I don't know. How could I? I just know I don't want to complicate your life any more than it is already, and that I don't like the way I'm behaving. I don't want to be a burden to you any more than you want to be a burden to me, or anyone else. I'm angry because you won't allow me to harvest grapevines on your land. It's left me with no routine to get through the day. Now the only thing I can rely on in my life are the afternoons I spend with Jason and Lacy. Every other hour of the day represents a challenge."

"Do you mind telling me what provoked this grand illumination?"

"Please don't be sarcastic. I was talking to Lacy about her mother not coming. Trying to explain how selfish Renie must be, how she wasn't looking outward to what Lacy's life was. I realized that where you're concerned, the same applied to me." She turned away from his probing eyes to set her glass on the mantel and stare down into the fire. "I feel so fenced in by my own emotions, I don't know which way to turn. All these years I've been taking care of Independent. Or trying to. He won't have it. He's fought me at every turn. Now I understand why. It's his life. I can't stop worrying about him, but that's my problem, not his."

"He's fine at the moment, if that'll ease your mind."

Kaley gaped. "You went up there? You talked to him?"

"He's on Rutledge land. I flanked him, had a look and left him alone. He didn't see me. The old mule was down and chuffing. I expect she's gone by now."

"I hope he doesn't sit up there and grieve himself to death." She heard herself and laughed with self-deprecation. "See what I mean? I want him back here for Christmas, but that's selfish. He's known Flossie longer than he's known me. He has a right to his grief. I don't know why I can't leave things well enough alone, why I always have to force the issues." Her legs were feeling rubbery. She sank down on a three-legged log stool, obviously built by Slater for the kids. She looked at him, a beseeching light in her eyes. "I guess what I came over here to say is that I want to be in your life. I want you in mine. If you can live one tomorrow at a time, so can I."

Her outpouring shook him. Her profile was delineated by the blaze so that it appeared a special light emanated from her. She wore a sweater and jeans tucked into soft, low-heeled boots. He admired the rounded curve of her shoulder, the slender column of her neck, the incurving line from hip to waist. The flickering light caught at the wisps of hair that had escaped her braid. Her jacket lay next to him on the sofa. It gave off her scent. He smoothed it out.

"Are you wanting me to say that I've been selfish, too?"

Not turning, she shook her head. "No. You've been truthful. I guess I just don't like knowing the truth. It hurts. If I were in your position, I'd do the same thing. Or maybe I wouldn't. You're not selfish at all.

"And anyway," she said, exhausted suddenly, as if she hadn't slept in weeks. "Permanency isn't the issue here. Who knows? On my way home I could slip off the path into the gully and break my neck."

He snapped his cigar into the fire. "Stay put a minute." He went into the kids' bedroom. Jason was soundly asleep, curled amid the battleground of trucks and soldiers and Lego. He ran his hand beneath the boy, checking for toys.

Lacy was on her back, snoring softly. Georgia, also on her back, was lying beside Lacy. The dog lifted its head. He scratched her behind the ears.

He moved silently back into the living room. Kaley was as he'd left her, still on the stool, her gaze fixed on space. She was so beautiful that just looking at her made his bones ache.

"Another drink?" he asked.

"No, I'm feeling the effects of the first one."

"Brandy's not for chugalugging."

"Look who's talking."

"Did you bank the fireplace before you came?"

She glanced at him. "Yes, why?"

"Leave anything in the oven?"

She shook her head.

"No early appointments? Now or in the near future?"

Her throat closed up. "Wha—"

She stared at him transfixed for so long, he thought he'd have to repeat himself, but finally he saw clarity lighting her eyes.

"Slater!" she cried softly and launched herself into his open arms.

He closed them about her so tightly she was immobilized.

AGES LATER he sat on the side of the bed watching her sleep. Her chestnut-colored hair, free from the restraining braid, was almost black against the pillow, and it partially obscured her face.

"You're what I always dreamed about, when I had the right to dream," he murmured.

She sighed deeply in her sleep, shifting so that the hair fell away from her face.

He lifted her hand and pressed his lips into her palm. When her eyes opened he smiled into them.

"What time is it?"

"After midnight. The beginning of Christmas Eve."

She stretched languidly. "It's funny, but I never think of it as being Christmas Eve until after supper." She turned her head to look out the bank of windows. "Will it snow, you think?"

"There's a snowflake or two falling out there now." He stroked her forehead. "Why the frown?"

"Just thinking about Independent. Those rocks are treacherous, especially coming down." She raised up on her elbows. "How are we going to work this? Will you and the kids come over to my place for Christmas dinner?"

"How about we spend Christmas Eve with you and Christmas here? Despite my reputation for canned pork and beans, I did buy a gargantuan ham, which only requires a few hours in the oven. And, if you would, you can take Lacy and Jason off my hands a few hours. I've still got to put their bicycles together. Every time I think I've got a few minutes to myself in the barn, they're at my heels. I'm surprised they haven't found the crates." He winced and rubbed his temple.

Kaley's chest went tight. "Headache?"

He didn't want to admit it. "Lack of sleep."

She lifted the bed covers. "Get in here then and get some."

He stretched out beside her, feeling the reactions start in his belly and whisper along his spine. He slid his arm beneath her shoulders. "Ahhh, missy. Who needs sleep?"

Chapter Fourteen

"You're positive you can see his smoke?" Kaley shaded her eyes from the swirling snowflakes as she gazed toward the top of Crosswind Ridge.

Slater guided her gaze. "He's had a fire going all day. Look off to your right a bit. There."

She gave up. "I don't see a thing. I'll have to take your word for it."

"You want me to go up there and bring him down?"

"No way. He's got his shotgun. He's liable to fill you full of buckshot."

He put his hand around her waist, looking at her with open affection. She leaned into his embrace, feeling loved and secure. She wanted to tell him how much she loved him, how afraid she was for him, but under the new rules both topics were taboo. "Your after-shave is turning me on," she said instead.

"Isn't it nice we have a good excuse to put Jason and Lacy to bed early tonight?"

"They won't sleep a wink and you know it. They're beside themselves with excitement."

"That's odd." He opened his jacket and drew her against his hips. "So am I."

She put her arms around his neck. His breath on her forehead was like a soft down feather. "I think the turkey has cooled down enough to slice by now."

"You have the damnedest way of changing a subject."

"One appetite at a time."

"Georgia won't come out from under the front porch," Lacy cried, her voice reaching them before she careened around the corner of the back porch.

Kaley stepped out of Slater's arms.

"I'll go cut off a turkey wing. She'll come out for that."

But she wouldn't. Slater used a flashlight to peer beneath the house while Jason and Lacy stayed near, hopping with anxiety.

"She's gone behind the chimney base."

Jason got down on his stomach. "I can crawl under there and bring her out."

"Maybe she's sick," Lacy said, beginning to cry. "I know she wouldn't hide from me on purpose."

"Okay, son." Slater gave the boy the flashlight. Jason wriggled under the steps and snaked his way toward the dog. Georgia growled.

Lacy lay prone in the snow. "What do you see? Is she okay?"

Jason's answer came to them garbled. He began squiggling backward. When his feet came in sight, Slater grabbed his ankles, tugging him the rest of the way out.

"She's having her puppies!" Jason said excitedly, swiping at the cobwebs, dirt and dead leaves clinging to his jacket. "I saw one. She was licking it."

Lacy insisted they move only on tiptoe around the house. Furniture had to be rearranged so she could lie over the spot above where Slater judged Georgia to be. She kept her ear pressed to the floorboards. "I can hear them squeaking," she whispered.

In the subdued quiet they all heard the car drive into the yard. Slater looked at Kaley. "You expecting company?"

"No one." She glided in stockinged feet to the window and peered out, recognizing at once the long nose of Miss Broom's old Packard. Miss Broom was already emerging from the driver's side and going around to open the passenger door. "It's Miss Broom, and she has someone with her. They're making a Christmas call."

Or perhaps Miss Broom had some information about Slater's opals! Kaley rushed outside.

"Goodness, girl. What're you doing running about barefoot? Never mind. Look who I collected from the bus station. Wilhelmina Rutledge, meet Kaley Jackson." She gave her arm to the woman in the car. "See, I told you if Slater wasn't home, he'd probably be here."

The elderly woman emerging from the Packard was thin as spaghetti, elegantly attired and newly permed. "I thought you had a broken leg," Kaley blurted.

Wilhelmina Rutledge grinned. "Still do." She lifted her skirt to display a walking cast. "But I wasn't going to let it keep me from spending Christmas with the only family I have left. Law'!" she said. "This is the first time I've set foot on Crosswind in better than thirty years. Takes me back, it does.'' She looked past Kaley and spied Slater coming down the steps. ''There you are, boy. What're you doing gallivanting around on Christmas Eve, leaving me to hitch a ride?''

''Bloody hell!'' he cursed, greeting his aunt by scooping her up and carrying her into the house over her laughing protests.

The next few minutes were chaos. Slater was angrily demanding why she'd come on the bus and hadn't let him know, while Lacy shouted ''Shh'' and refused to budge off the floor, which had to be explained. Jason sat happily at Aunt Willie's feet and got inspected from head to toe while Aunt Willie chatted on about having to call the only friend she had left in Fentress County for a ride, because Slater was nowhere near his telephone. And where was that old blowhard, Independent? Slater'd said he was still alive, but she had to see him for herself before she'd believe it.

Ascertaining amid the cacophony of everyone trying to talk at once that the newcomers would stay for supper, Kaley retreated to the kitchen to get out of the babble and add place settings to the table.

Miss Broom soon followed.

''Monumental luck, my dear,'' she said. ''Lacy apparently dropped the opals as the class let out. Miss Henderson found them and put them in her desk drawer. She about nearly had a heart attack when I told her about them. Despite Lacy's insistence, she had no idea they were quite so valuable.''

She removed the chamois from her purse and deposited it on the table.

Kaley hugged the elderly woman. "You're a lifesaver. Slater would've been crushed if these had been lost forever."

"I would've been what?" he said, entering the kitchen. Kaley froze. Miss Broom did an about-face. "I'll just see if Willie needs any help freshening up. It was just luck she caught me. I was on my way to church."

Slater's gaze alighted on the chamois. His face paled. "What the hell—"

"I can explain."

His eyes glinted with restrained rage. "Why don't you do just that, missy."

"Could you reserve judgment for a moment?"

His eyes locked with hers as he leaned against the doorjamb. "I'll give it a moment."

She opened the chamois and tilted the stones onto the table. "Are they all there?"

He glanced at them. "Yes."

She scooped them up and put them back into the bag. "I don't want to tell you how they came to be here. First, because I made a promise, and second, because someone else needs to do the explaining."

"Am I to understand you knew the opals were missing, and you now want to be honorable at my expense?"

"I couldn't have said it better myself." There was no mistaking his rising wrath. "Give me a minute, okay?" She brushed past him and went to get Lacy. Miss Broom and Aunt Willie were disappearing down the hall toward the bathroom, Aunt Willie's walking cast clunking on the floor. Jason was lying next to Lacy.

"Miss Broom found the opals," she told her.

Lacy gasped. "I'll put them back as soon as I get home."

Kaley shook her head. "It's too late for that. Slater has seen them. You're going to have to tell him what you've done."

Lacy blanched. "Come with me?"

"I'm sorry sweetheart, but you're going to have to do this on your own."

"I told you you'd get us into trouble," Jason said, catching his sister's fear.

Kaley pointed Lacy toward the kitchen. "Go on. It won't be as bad as you think."

At the kitchen door, Lacy looked back. Kaley gave her a weak, but encouraging smile. She sat on the floor with Jason.

"I bet he spanks her, or makes us go back to Atlanta with Aunt Willie."

"Let's hope not. And Aunt Willie is going to live here with all of you."

Jason shook his head. "Nuh-uh. Aunt Willie said she's just here for a bit."

"Oh? When did she say that?"

"When I asked her," he said ambiguously. He put his ear back to the floor. "I wonder how many puppies Georgia has now?"

Kaley lingered a moment, but curiosity got the best of her. She headed back to the kitchen and stood in the doorway. Slater was sitting on a chair, his hands at Lacy's waist while she stood between his knees and stared at her feet.

He looked up and saw Kaley.

"Okay," he said to Lacy, "that'll do for now. I'll decide on a punishment later."

"Are you going to send me to an orphanage?"

"Where in heck did you get an idea like that?"

"That's what Daddy always said when we weren't good."

Kaley watched Slater's face go rigid. "He did, eh? Well I'm keeping you around so I can make your life miserable when you misbehave. Go on and see how Georgia is doing."

Kaley stepped back around the corner to allow Lacy to pass. "Was it bad?" she whispered.

Lacy made a grimace Slater couldn't see. "Nah."

He sat for a long moment with his hands folded and dipped between his knees. "Jerome always was a bully. It's pretty damned lousy to threaten impressionable kids that way, especially after their mother has already done a bounder. Better to take a switch to their behinds and be done with it."

"You're not going to spank her?"

"No. My momma raised me not to hit girls. I'm going to make her muck out the barn for the rest of her life."

"You're a softie!"

He palmed the chamois full of opals. "Good God! It's only hitting me now what a loss these would've been."

"They weren't lost, just misplaced."

"Soon as the bank opens Monday, I'm going to rent a safe-deposit box. And I guess when school reopens I'll have to break down and go talk to a bunch of fourth graders."

"You're larger than life to Lacy and Jason. You can imagine how they must sound talking about you at school. Sometimes I can't believe you're for real myself." Her sigh turned into a shudder. "It'd be nice if we could box up and store everything we love for safekeeping, wouldn't it?"

"Are you going melancholy on me?"

She dredged up a smile. "Holiday blues. Doc Fuller hasn't been in touch has he?"

Slater rose from the chair. "No."

"Can't you even let yourself hope?" she cried, anguish threading her voice.

"No," he answered truthfully. Then, more quietly, "No."

"Are you angry with me?" She kept her distance, afraid that she had wrecked everything.

"Very."

She unwrapped a package of rolls and began lining them up on a pan, the activity a bridge from despair to the ordinary. "Your aunt will like what you've done to the house, don't you think?"

"I think we'll get supper out of the way. Then I'll take Aunt Willie and the kids home and put them to bed. While I'm gone you get rid of Miss Broom. And once my blood pressure drops to normal, I'll come back here and chastise you for keeping a promise that almost put me in the poorhouse."

"Chastise me?" A tingle of excitement started up inside her. "What did you have in mind?"

"Believe me, missy, it won't be mucking out the barn."

CHRISTMAS MORNING dawned postcard-perfect. The sun was rising on a dusting of pristine snow that upholstered the ground in a layer of fluffy white. The air was cold and tender. Independent's smoke trailed visibly into the sky, so Kaley retreated into the living room for her morning coffee.

Beneath her feet she could hear the puppies mewling and squeaking. Kaley smiled. Birth, rebirth and joy. That was what today was all about. Oddly, she wasn't feeling anything but sad.

Last night had been wonderful when Slater had returned. They'd made love against the backdrop of twinkling tree lights and the cinnamon-scented fire, whispered love nothings and shared cocoa before he left for home to get a few hours sleep before Santa had to spread toys beneath the tree.

The awful part was waking up alone on Christmas day.

She ached with the desire to have her own family, to be opening presents, taking pictures, sitting around in red Christmas robes while turkey and yams baked.

And good manners dictated that she wait until at least noon before she went up to Slater's where Aunt Willie was now the appointed hostess.

She was pouring herself a second cup of coffee when she heard her name being called.

Lacy was barreling down the path on her new bike, cutting a trail of wobbly tracks that would've done justice to a drunken boa constrictor. Kaley went out onto the porch.

"Merry Christmas!" she called, her mood lifting.

Lacy grinned, braked and shot off the bike, leaving it lying in the snow.

"Aunt Willie said I could come down and see Georgia."

"She did? What's Slater up to?"

"He had to go somewhere. Aunt Willie said for you to come up to the house soon's you can."

"Is something wrong?"

"She can't stand on her feet all day to cook. She's wantin' help. And anyway Slater told her you would." She threw open her coat. "Look. I wore my oldest clothes. Can I have the flashlight and go under the house to see the puppies?"

Kaley sipped her coffee. "I hate to say no."

"Then, don't. Please."

"Well. That's a new word in your vocabulary."

Lacy's cheeks went pink. "I gotta see the puppies, Kaley."

"All right. I'll make up a bowl of leftovers for Georgia. Where's Jason? Didn't he want to come?"

"He doesn't know how to ride his bike yet. He's waiting for Slater to put the training wheels on."

An hour later Lacy ecstatically regaled Aunt Willie with the particulars of Georgia's litter while Kaley lifted the bike down from the bed of her truck.

"Three brown, one red, one white and two black! They're so tiny. And Georgia let me touch them!"

"Seven! Goodness me," Aunt Willie said, smiling over at Kaley as she pulled her sweater tight around her thin shoulders. She wore one of Slater's socks over her cast. "I'm glad you could come, child. I meant to tell you last night not to let an old bag like me interfere with what you've established here, but I'm afraid I got carried away catching up on thirty years of gossip with Thelma."

Kaley propped the bike against the porch. "I don't know that I have anything established. I've been helping out where I could—with the kids."

"Oh, more than that. All I've heard is 'Kaley said.'"

Kaley laughed. "All *I've* heard is 'Aunt Willie said.' For the longest I thought your *name* was Aunt Willie said."

"Does my heart good to see Slater content. First time I've ever seen him so unfidgety. Except for this morning. He got a call and shot out of here like his tail was on fire. I thought perhaps it was you who called."

"It wasn't me." So...who? Surely not Dr. Fuller, not on Christmas day.

Putting her mind on something else, she returned to the truck and filled her arms with Christmas presents.

Willie held open the door for her, but once Kaley was across the threshold, she stayed at her post. "Now where's that scamp, Jason?"

"COME ON outten them bushes, boy. It ain't the polite thing to sneak up on a fellow woodsman."

Jason parted the bushes, dousing himself with damp snow.

"I wasn't sneakin'. I know who you are. You're Independent Jackson, Kaley's grampa."

"Waal, ain't you the clever one. And you'd be one of them Rutledge scoundrels."

"Uncle Slater is the scoundrel. I'm not old enough. I'm only five."

"You cold?"

"A little bit."

Independent pointed toward the end of the log with his whittling knife. "Sit there. Warm a spell."

Jason eyed the knife. "I'm not supposed to talk to strangers."

"That a fact? Don't reckon I count as a stranger. You know my Kaley and I knew your grampa and his pa afore him. We use to do a fair amount of huntin' together. Course, animals is scarce now. An' them what's left ain't hardly worth the bullet."

"You did?" Jason stepped out from the shrubs and sat gingerly on the end of the log. "Did you know my dad?"

"Nope, never paid much attention to tads until they was outta long dresses. Fire won't reach that far. Git closer, boy. I ain't gonna bite."

Jason moved an inch.

Independent pulled a plug of tobacco from his pocket, sliced off a piece and stuck it in his jaw. He looked at Jason. "Want a neighborly chew?"

Jason reared back. "No way. Tobacco causes cancer. My face might fall off."

"You believe all that hooey? I been chewin' better'n seventy years and my face ain't fell off yet."

"It looks like it's ready to. It's awful wrinkled."

Independent rubbed a palm over his week-old beard. "Those're life lines, boy. Got a wrinkle for every inch I traveled." He worked the tobacco until it was soft cud, and spit a brown stream into the fire where it hissed pleasantly.

"Kaley's been watching for your smoke every morning. Me and Lacy help."

"Never have knowed a woman more aggravatin'. If she can't find somethin' handy to worry over, she'd sew it or grow it. Speakin' of which, she's got the same idea on tobaccy you do. This here plug is our little secret."

"Did Flossie die?"

Independent stared at the sky. "Sad to say, she did, son."

"Did she cry?"

He turned a sharp eye on Jason. "Waal, now. I can't say she did, and can't say she didn't."

"Where is she?"

"Yonder, in a brush layabout."

"Are you going to just leave her there?"

"Reckon so. It's a nice spot, full of laurel. She can keep her back to the wind. What brings you up this way all alone? Ye running away from home?"

"No sir! I love living here. I already built me a fort, and Uncle Slater's gonna build me a tree house. I'm going to heaven to see my dad. I got him a Christmas present."

Independent stopped working his chew. "Do tell?"

Jason sighed. "Do you know the way? I've been climbing all morning."

"Truth to tell, I have to think on it. What's the present?"

"I'll show you." Jason shrugged out of his book bag and put it between his knees to open it. The present was haphazardly folded into red tissue. He carefully peeled the paper away. "It's a wind chime." He held it up. "Hear that? When the wind blows on the sticks they make music. It's awful hard to buy something for somebody who's in heaven. Uncle Slater said folks in heaven have all they really need." He sighed heavily. "I was gonna buy him a shirt, but I didn't have enough money. Do you think they have Christmas in heaven?''

Independent stared off into space. ''I reckon they do.''

Jason rewrapped the chimes. ''Which way do I go from here?''

''As I recollect, we're in the foothills of heaven right here.'' He watched the boy's eyes widen.

''For real?''

''Of course, for real! I ain't of a mind to lie to a tad like you.'' He spit a stream into the fire, listened while it hissed.

''I didn't mean you told lies.''

''Fair enough. But I suspect the good Lord ain't gonna let you go no farther than a few more yards up that deer trail yonder.'' He pointed with his knife. ''Like as not, if you was to hang that contraption from a pine bough, your pa'd hear it just fine.''

Jason stood up, hesitant. ''You want to go with me?''

The old throat gave out a cracked laugh. ''I better not, son. Seems like I been on a path t'other direction. Anyway, the Lord might take one look at me and figure I'm ripe for takin', which I ain't just yet. You go on. There's a squatty pine you can reach just fine. I'll wait here and take ye down to home. I was just sittin' here waitin' for an excuse to break camp anyways.''

Chapter Fifteen

Doc Fuller met him at the clinic door. "Hated to pull you away from family on Christmas morning, but the boy is only going to be here today."

Slater shook Fuller's hand. "What boy are we talking about?"

"The ace neuropathologist. Didn't I mention? He's my son."

"Seems you forgot to tell me that."

"Don't get riled. He's so damned smart, I can't believe it myself sometimes. When I tell folks he's mine, they compare him to me and short him. Which is damned unfair. This way."

He led Slater into a small room littered with crayons and stuffed toys. "Light's better in here."

The son turned from the window where he'd been holding up a sheet of X rays. He thrust out his hand. "I'm Frank." He barreled on while still examining the X rays. "I tried to talk Dad into waiting to call you tomorrow, but he's got it in his mind you might consider this a Christmas present."

Slater felt himself stop breathing. "Why?"

"Come here and look." Frank pointed to the largest of the X rays. "I enlarged this myself. There's your tumor." He pointed with a pencil.

Slater let out his breath. It wasn't to be good news, after all. "I see it."

"Yes, well, look at this. See this white spot? That's a calcium deposit. It's not supposed to be there. Dad said you had an infection and he's been feeding you antibiotics. Looks like the infection reached your brain, which is a damned hard thing to do, but the antibiotics got to it and the drainage off the infection just sort of pooled right there. That's what's forming calcium."

"I'm worse off," Slater said tiredly.

Frank looked at him. "Hell, no, man. That calcium deposit is sitting square on the blood vessel that's feeding the tumor. My best guess is that a month or six weeks from now, when you have another set of pictures made, I won't find any hint of tumor. In layman's language, it's starving to death, drying up. Poof."

Slater locked his knees so that they wouldn't buckle on him. "What's the snag?" he asked, oddly aware of the workings of his throat and tongue to produce the words.

"There is some fluid on the brain. Some of it's going into that calcium deposit. The rest, for the moment, is draining into the spinal column. That ought to be checked once a year. If it ever stops draining on its own, you'd be looking at having a shunt put in to facilitate the drainage. The calcium deposit isn't going to cause you any distress. I've studied war casualties with bullets and shrapnel lodged in their brains. They function just fine."

Doc Fuller put a hand on Slater's shoulder. "C'mon, son, I'll walk you out. You look like you could use the fresh air. Frank, you get along home to your mama. She's waitin' breakfast for you."

Slater shook the young man's hand. "Thanks."

"My pleasure."

Outside the office, the air had a crisp bite to it. Slater inhaled deeply.

"I charge double for holiday office visits."

Slater grinned politely and handed over two cigars. "I'll see to it you get a case."

"I'll hold you to that." Fuller pocketed one and peeled the other, holding it beneath his nose, sniffing the rich aroma. "Hand rolled, aren't they?"

"My one indulgence." Slater couldn't believe they were talking about cigars when his death sentence had just been lifted.

"By the by, you wouldn't by any chance be kin to the Rutledge in Miss Henderson's fourth grade?"

Slater frowned. "Lacy? Yes."

"Well, tell her to lay off my grandson, Billy Snow. She's filling his head full of treasure huntin' and adventure. I got down-to-earth plans for that boy."

"I'll tell her." He clasped Doc Fuller's hand. "There's a creek runs across my land. Seems like it's got some pan-size bream in it, if you're ever interested in popping a fly."

"First chance I get. I'll bring Billy if that's all right with you."

"Fine." He hesitated. "Merry Christmas."

"You, too, son. *Lots* of 'em. You fit to drive, now? For a second or two I thought you were goin' to faint on us in there."

Slater grinned. "For a second or two, *I* thought I was going to faint on you."

"This kinda made my day."

Slater laughed. "It damned sure made mine."

AUNT WILLIE AND KALEY and Lacy were standing on the front porch waiting for him, so that for one anxious minute, Slater thought they knew where he'd been and had learned the news.

"We can't find Jason," Kaley said the moment he alighted from his truck. "We've looked everywhere, checked all the gullies between here and my house, both barns. I went up on the slate run..."

"Shh, missy." He put his arm around her shoulders, battling the instinct to take her fully into his arms and whisper wonderful things into her ear. "We'll find him. He's got a fort up the hill behind the barn, maybe—"

"It was the first place I looked," Lacy told him.

"It's all my fault," Willie said dispiritedly. "He slipped out while I was having my coffee and daydreaming about—" Her eyes shifted suddenly to a point beyond Slater and Kaley, toward the edge of the clearing. "Well, bless my soul," she breathed, and clunked down the steps.

Kaley and Slater turned.

Independent was emerging from the forest, and he had Jason by the hand.

Willie was hobbling out to meet them. "Indy Jackson, is that you? Law'! You look about a thousand years old." She stopped a few yards from him and sniffed. "Smell like it, too. Why, you've been up in that old cave. I can smell polecat musk on you."

"Dern. What hole did you sprout from? I thought I run ye off good and tight."

"Hah! You ain't run me nowhere. What a mess you are! Was Sary to get a look at you, she'd turn over in her grave."

"We've been up in the foothills of heaven," Jason said. "And next week Independent is going to take me to an auction. I'm goin' to help him pick out another mule."

Mortified, Independent released Jason's hand as if it were poison. "Stop runnin' off at the mouth, boy." He turned to go. Willie grabbed a handful of jacket.

"Where you running off to? Come into the kitchen and sit a spell. We've got a mite to catch up on."

"I'm not setting foot in a Rutledge house."

"Yes, you are, you ornery old goat." She dragged him along.

"Git your claws off me!"

She ignored his outburst. "You always were one for the long pout. Thirty years about takes the cake. I mind it's time to serve you up some crow and make you eat it. Help me up these steps. Your manners have gone to hell in a hand basket." Without a backward glance, she gestured toward those standing in the yard. "You young folks go play for an hour or so."

Lacy and Jason took her at her word and raced toward the barn.

Slater was laughing softly. "Poor old guy, he never had a chance. Never saw a man's wings clipped quite so neatly." He glanced down at Kaley. Tears were running down her cheeks. "C'mon, love, what's all this?"

"I've never seen Independent so meek. And did you see the way he was holding Jason's hand? Maybe he's found an even better replacement for Flossie."

He kissed away the salty tears on her cheeks, then slipped his arm beneath her jacket and around her waist. "Aunt Willie has the right idea. Let's go play—at your house. I have an urge to see you naked—"

She caught the undercurrent of excitement in his voice. "Where've you been? We were frantic—"

"I'll get to that later."

She balked. "Now."

"Later." His hand crept up her back beneath her sweater.

"Stop that! Your hand is cold."

"It'll warm up soon enough. You still interested in harvesting grapevines on Rutledge land?"

"Of course I'm interested!"

"You'd have to become a Rutledge."

"Well, that's—*what?*"

She stumbled on the path.

Slater righted her.

"Maybe have a baby or two."

Her fingertips were buzzing, her throat closed up, her knees and ankles seemed not to want to support her.

Slater glanced at her. "I know the feeling," he commiserated.

Without missing a stride, he picked her up and upended her over his shoulder.

"Oh, damn. Slater! Not again. Put me down."

"Nope."

"This is silly."

With a sense of place, he looked at trees shawled in snow, the little dirt lane zigzagging off in search of adventure, the hills of crumpled velvet, and the weeds that had yellowed in the first frost.

She yanked at his hair.

"Let me go!"

He smiled.

"Now, missy, I'm *never* going to do that."

COMING NEXT MONTH

EXTREME JUSTICE Marilyn Tracy

It had been three years since FBI agent John Chandler had saved Kelsey's life. Now she was in danger again—and John's assignment was to guard her with his life. But Kelsey refused to need anyone—including John.

CHRISTMAS EVERY DAY Marie Ferrarella

The final part of a delightful trilogy featuring the Sinclair family.

Nik Sinclair needed a temporary accountant—and fancy-free Sara seemed just right. But Sara was running from something... Life had taught her that nothing wonderful ever lasted—and she knew her feelings for Nik meant it was time to move on...

LADY OF THE NIGHT Emilie Richards

Jane Doe wasn't just another patient. Mystery surrounded her...and Joshua found himself completely entranced with the amnesiac woman whom he called Maggie...

NO RETREAT Marilyn Pappano

He Who Dares

As a child, Riley Cooper had been the troublemaker from the wrong side of town. Now he *was* the law—and he'd just arrested the young son of Liza Davis, the woman who'd once thought herself too good for him...